fractured
lines

an *Out of Line* novel

fractured

lines

an *Out of Line* novel

Jen McLaughlin

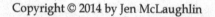

Print ISBN: 978-0-9896684-9-1

The author acknowledges the copyrighted or trademarked status and trademark owners of all the wordmarks mentioned in this work of fiction.

Edited by: Kristin at Coat of Polish Edits
Copy edited by: Hollie Westring
Cover Designed by: Sarah Hansen at © OkayCreations.net
Interior Design and Formatting by: E.M. Tippetts Book Designs

Books by
Jen McLaughlin

Out of Line Series:
Out of Line
Out of Time
Out of Mind

Between Us

Written as Diane Alberts:

Take a Chance Series:
Try Me (Take a Chance #1)
Love Me (Take a Chance #2)
Play Me (Take a Chance #3)
Take Me (Take a Chance #4)

Falling for the Groomsman
Faking It
Divinely Ruined
On One Condition
Broken
Kiss Me At Midnight
Kill Me Tomorrow
Temporarily Yours
Reclaimed

Superstars in Love Series:
Captivated by You
One Night

The lines we once crossed so easily have widened and torn us apart...

Once upon a time I thought Finn and I would live happily ever after, but real life doesn't always have a happy ending. He's testing my trust, and I'm losing faith in the man I thought I'd spend the rest of my life with, and there's nothing I do can stop it. He's the one I trusted to keep me safe, but now he's the source of my greatest pain...

Forgiveness is fragile, and some fractures never fully heal...

One mistake—a slip in a moment of weakness—might cost me everything I've worked so hard for. The thing about trust is that it's a lot easier to lose than it is to build. Just as I'm about to give up and surrender to the demons from my past, an unexpected threat reminds me what I'm best at: protecting the woman I love. Whether or not she wants me, I will fight for Carrie and our daughter, and I will keep them safe—no matter the cost.

Even if I have to put my life and my heart on the line.

An Excerpt from Fractured Lines...

I lowered my face even more. "I need you so damn bad. Let me kiss you. Let me make it better. I know how to make it all better."

I brushed my lips across hers gently, testing her reaction. She kissed me back. So soft I barely felt it, and yet I somehow felt it down to my soul.

With a small groan, I closed my mouth over hers, crushing her against my chest and holding her so tightly I might have broken a rib. Man, I'd been waiting for this moment. For her to stop shutting me out. For her to want me as much as I needed her.

And now it was happening.

I slanted my mouth over hers, taking full control of the kiss. Backing her up against the wall, my tongue glided inside her mouth at the same time I slipped my leg in between hers. She gasped and opened her mouth wider, granting me full access.

Without hesitation, I took it, and then I took some more.

Like the greedy asshole I really was.

Part of me knew I should stop kissing her until I was better, but the other part of me wanted her too damn badly to give a shit about anything else. When I closed my hands around her hips, my fingers digging into the soft sides of her ass, she broke off the kiss and took a shaky breath.

I latched onto her neck, biting with just enough pressure to sting. It had been too long since I'd had her. Too long since I'd held her. Too long for everything. My injured leg protested against the weight I put on it, but I ignored the cry of protest it gave. Any pain I had to suffer was worth it, as long as Carrie was in my arms again, making those small sounds that drove me fucking insane.

"I need you." I hauled her leg up around my waist, pressing my cock against her hot pussy. "I need you naked, screaming, and crying out my name. *Now.*"

This one goes out to all the Finn and Carrie fans out there.
This one's for you.

chapter
one

Carrie

At seven o'clock sharp, I closed the door behind my last patient of the day, collapsed against it, and removed my glasses, swiping my forearm across my forehead while letting out an exhausted sigh. It had been a longer day than usual, probably because of how incredibly crappy I felt.

I'd thrown up three times today, and I had a feeling I was about to do it a fourth. All I wanted was to get home to my husband and my daughter, take a hot shower, and crawl into bed. Finn would be there waiting for me with a smile and a hug, and Susan would babble happily as I walked in the door. God, I needed that right now.

Pushing off the door, I swiped my hands on my pencil skirt and crossed the room, my mind solely fixed on home. I'd been working extra hours the past two weeks, fitting in more patients for some extra cash. I'd been happily married to my husband, Finn, for three years, and life couldn't be better…but he'd been home from work for the past few days because he'd been in a car accident.

The doctor wouldn't clear him to go back for at least another six days. For both of our sakes, I hoped those six days passed quickly. He needed to get back to work. He'd been restless and shaky lately. Finn had never done well with inactivity, and this was no exception. He needed to get back to normal.

And so did I.

I gathered my phone, MacBook Air, and notebook off my desk. As I shoved the phone into my purse, it lit up. I picked it up, narrowing my eyes when I saw it was the pharmacy calling. I hadn't called anything in, so why would they be calling me now?

"Hello?" I said, juggling my bag and my briefcase and the phone on my shoulder.

"Mrs. Coram?"

"Yes, this is she." I headed for the door, shutting the light off as I went. "How can I help you?"

"This is Trish from Good Health Pharmacy. I'm calling about your husband's prescription." I could hear the smile in her voice. That's how cheerful this woman sounded. She had no idea the dread her words sent through me, or how much she was about to ruin my life. "It's ready to be picked up. I tried calling him too, but it went right to voicemail. I understand he's in a lot of pain, so I figured I'd try to catch you."

My bags hit the floor, and so did my internal organs.

Finn had been in an accident, but he'd refused pain medication. He hadn't wanted to tempt a relapse since he'd once used the pills to self-medicate his way out of PTSD all those years ago. Back when we'd been dating, and he'd been a Marine. Long story short, his unit had been ambushed, and he'd been the only one to survive. After that, he hadn't been the same. It had taken him months to feel normal again, and part of that process had involved pain pills, sleepless nights, and a breakup.

He'd told me he didn't trust himself to go down that road again, and that he'd just take off work for a few weeks and recover. When I'd asked him if he was sure, he'd smiled and said, "Positive as a proton, Ginger."

I'd believed him.

"Mrs. Coram? Are you there?"

I snapped out of my shock, gripping the phone. "Yes. I'm sorry."

"Will you be picking them up tonight? We close at nine."

"Yes. I'll be there in a few minutes," I said, trying to keep my tone steady, even though I wanted to scream at the top of my lungs. The last thing I needed was the local pharmacist thinking I was a banshee. "Thank you."

I hung up without waiting for a reply and collapsed against the wall, my breathing coming out uneven. Probably because of the piercing pain in my chest where my heart was supposed to be. He'd lied to me. Hidden the need for pain pills from me. Why? I could have helped him. I was here for him, no matter what.

Why had he felt the need to hide his pain from me?

I took a deep breath and tried to calm down. Maybe there was a perfectly logical explanation for this. Maybe it was a mistake. Maybe he hadn't slipped back into old habits, and he wasn't lying about taking pills again. Maybe my life, my *love*, wasn't crumbling around my feet all over again.

But then again, maybe it was.

Holding a hand to my stomach, I bolted for the bathroom. I barely made it in time. The contents of my stomach came hurling out *Exorcist* style, and by the time I was finished I shook uncontrollably. I'd been so worried that this accident might cause a relapse of sorts, especially since it had happened right around the anniversary of his father's death. But he'd seemed so strong. So invincible.

I'd had faith that he would come to me if he were having issues.

As a general rule, I tried to give him privacy when it came to his mental health. He'd married me for *me*, not because I was a therapist. The last thing he needed was me poking around in his brain, trying to analyze him and tell him how to fix himself. It would only cause unresolved hatred and anger. But maybe I'd given him too much space.

Maybe I'd missed the warning signs.

Hugging the toilet, scared to move, I closed my eyes and thought back. He hadn't been sleeping in bed with me, and had taken to sleeping on the couch with some football on in the background, but I'd thought it was due to the lack of pain pills, and the impossibility to sleep well with me rolling around kicking him in my sleep. Maybe I'd been wrong. Maybe it was something else entirely.

And I hadn't known it.

With shaking legs, I made my way to the car. The whole time I drove to the pharmacy, my mind went a million miles a minute. I thought of how he'd started acting more jittery a week or so ago. How he'd been flushed when I came home every day instead of pale. And his shifty eyes when I'd asked him how the pain was.

He'd been more active, too, instead of resting. I'd thought it had been a good sign of his improvement. Instead, it might have been the first indicator of his downfall.

How had I missed it?

Walking to the counter, I plastered a shaky smile on my face. "Hello. I'm picking up for Finn—er, Griffin Coram."

The pharmacist smiled and pulled the bag off the rung. "I'm glad I caught you before we closed. When he called earlier, he sounded as if he was really suffering. It took a few calls, but I managed to get his prescription refilled. Tell him to be more careful with his pills next time, and to keep track of where he put the bottle. I won't be able to get

3

an early refill again."

Early refills.

Just like the last time he'd been taking them.

Back then, I'd been the one making the phone calls for him. I'd have to make up excuses about missed pills and extreme pain. Now he was doing it again, behind my back. "How many refills has he had so far?"

"It's been three or four now, I think." The pharmacist studied me. "Is there a problem?"

I wanted to tell her not to give Finn any more meds, but I knew it was a Band-Aid fix. If I told her about his history, he'd just go somewhere else. Another doctor. Another pharmacy. The streets. I couldn't stop that. If he wanted to get better, well, he had to *want* to get better. I could help. I *would* help, but ultimately…

It would be up to him. And only him.

I forced a smile. I swore I heard my face crack. "I knew. I'm just trying to keep track of it all."

"Oh." She blinked. "Right."

She rang me out, and I made one more stop in aisle ten. By the time I walked outside, I felt like things had gone from bad to worse. The niggling suspicion in the back of my mind had been confirmed, and instead of filling me with joy, it terrified me.

My foundation was cracking, and there was nothing I could do to stop it. If Finn was lying to me again, hiding his problems from me again, then I knew from my work that there was only so much I could do. He had to want to help himself…

Or he'd have to go.

I'd forgiven him thousands of times for thousands of things, but this time was different. As much as I loved him—and I did, with *all* of my heart—he needed to get better. This wasn't just my heart and my emotions he was playing with.

We had a family now.

Everything had changed.

chapter
two

Finn

I rolled over on the cold, hard ground, the sound of someone crying breaking through the haze of sleep hovering over me. I'd been lying in this damned bloody field for hours, waiting for rescue. I'd been left for dead, and soon I would be. I just wished death would hurry his ass up, grab his scepter, and come claim me already.

I was ready.

The crying got louder, and I groaned. Hadn't everyone died yet? I'd thought I was the only one left here alive. Hell, Dotter had bled out in my arms hours ago. I'd tasted his blood on my tongue, in my throat, had it all over my face. I'd never forget that horror for as long as I lived.

Which, ironically enough, wouldn't be very long.

The crying continued, and I forced my eyes open. Instead of the dark, cloudy skies I remembered, I saw a white ceiling and heard the vague noises of a football game.

Blinking, I remembered. The attack had been years ago. I was home, alive and safe. I was no longer a Marine, but a computer engineer. I was happily married, with a lovely daughter. I wasn't dead. I was *alive*.

Sighing, my eyes drifted shut, and I fell back into slumber.

But the crying didn't stop...

5

Carrie

When I got home, I sat in my car for a minute, gripping the wheel so tightly my fingers ached. He should have told me, damn it.

If he'd come to me, and asked me to help him keep track of pills, this wouldn't be happening. I wouldn't be flashing back in time to a place I'd rather forget. To a time when Finn had fallen apart in front of my eyes.

And I'd had to let him go. I didn't want to let him go again. I didn't want to, but if it was better for my family, I *would*. I wanted to take care of him like I did before, yes.

But I had to take care of my daughter, too. Susan.

After taking a deep breath, I pushed the car door open, slamming it shut behind me, and made my way up the driveway. I opened the front door and studied the foyer, expecting to find Finn filling it with his presence, smiling at me like usual. Acting as if nothing was wrong. It was empty.

My heart twisted and sped up painfully. Why wasn't he there? Where was he? His rental had been out front, so he had to be here. "Finn?"

Nothing. Oh my God, what if he'd taken too many pills?

What if he was dead?

What if it wasn't just the pills? What if he'd been having flashbacks from his PTSD again? And, oh my God, what about Susan? Where was our daughter?

The possibilities were endless, and they all swam through my mind in vivid detail as I ran through the house frantically, checking each room. The kitchen was empty, where Finn should have been cooking dinner for us.

As was the dining room, where Susan should have been sitting in her high chair, eating her nighttime snack of Cheerios. I skidded into the living room, tears filling my eyes and sweat coating my palms.

The first thing I saw was Susan, awake and sitting up in her playpen. Her face was red, as if she'd been crying, and she rubbed her eyes sleepily. When she saw me, the look of relief in her eyes was equal parts disturbing and satisfying. She was alive and safe, which sent satisfaction shooting through me, but she'd been *crying*.

And Finn hadn't come to her side.

I forced my eyes off her for a second. The next thing I saw was Finn. He was prone on the couch, his head turned into the cushions so I couldn't see his face. For a horrible, terrifying second I thought he was dead.

But then he moved, scratching his cheek, and rolled onto his side. I let out a breath I hadn't known I'd been holding and picked up Susan, tears streaming down my face. A mixture of relief, anger, betrayal, and protectiveness warred within me—fighting with my concern for the man I loved.

He'd passed out, and neglected our child. Finn would never do that. Ever. Who was this man in my living room? Where was my Finn? And how could I get him back?

I walked into the kitchen, kissing Susan's forehead as I went. She tugged on my hair and snuggled close, rubbing her forehead against my cheek. Her universal sign for sleepiness. No wonder, since it was her bedtime. I surveyed the counters.

Nothing had changed from earlier, when I'd cleaned up after breakfast and gone to work. Finn had kissed me goodbye. Then what? He'd gotten high?

I swallowed hard and opened the dishwasher. The dishes were still clean, and the sink was empty. He hadn't cooked dinner.

He hadn't fed Susan her dinner, let alone a snack.

On the counter, a blank notepad sat next to the phone. Slowly, I walked to the trash can and stepped on the lever to open the lid. With one hand, I dug around a bit. Inside, buried underneath three plastic bags and tucked inside an empty can, I found the empty pill bottle. I found the evidence I'd known I would find, deep down in my soul.

He'd gotten high, stuck our thirteen-month-old in a playpen, and passed out. Anything could have happened. She could have climbed out and gotten into trouble. She was getting better at climbing. Or there could have been a fire. A burglar. An earthquake…

And he'd left Susan alone.

Who was he?

Forcing a calm breath, I kissed Susan's cheek and whispered, "It'll be okay. Don't worry. Everything is going to be okay."

Even though I knew it wasn't.

After I fed Susan and put her to bed, I checked on Finn again.

He was still asleep, and still breathing. I took the opportunity to search the truck he'd rented after the accident, and found another empty bottle in his glove box, hidden under a few pamphlets. Each discovery I made hurt even more than the last. I knew what I would say to a client, and I knew how I would counsel someone else, but I was lost here.

This was my husband.

I'd been nothing but supportive to him for the last eight years, and this is what I got in return? More lies and secrets? I didn't know what my next step should be. What the best thing for all of us would be. I didn't just have me to think about. I pressed a hand to my stomach and swallowed hard. I had to think about our family.

Not him. Not me.

Shakily, I sat down next to the couch and waited. After what seemed like years later, he finally woke up. He rolled over and saw me sitting there, and for a second, I saw the worry cross his face. For a second, I saw the panic.

But then he smiled that seductive smile of his. "Hey, Ginger. You're home."

"Yeah." I forced a small smile. "Tired?"

"I guess so. The pain got to be a bit much, so I needed a refresher." He sat up and scrubbed his hand down his face, and craned his neck toward the empty playpen. "Susan was napping in her playpen, so I laid down, too. Is she still asleep? You must be home early."

"It's eight thirty at night," I said slowly. "I've been home for more than an hour."

"Oh, shit." He stood up, his face blanching. "I'm so sorry. I must've been more tired than I thought. I'm so sorry. So, so sorry."

"Sh." I reached out and grabbed his hand, squeezing it. "It's okay." Even though it wasn't.

"It's not." He paced back and forth, his limp more pronounced. As he tugged on his hair, his steps growing more and more agitated with each movement, I stayed quiet, willing him to come forward with the truth. Silently begging him to tell me the truth. "I didn't sleep well last night, and it caught up with me."

"Are you in too much pain?" I laced my fingers together. "Do you need to call the doctor for some pills? I could help you with it. Keep track of times, or whatever."

I held my breath and angled my body toward his. This was his last chance to be honest. His last opportunity to show me he'd changed. That he wouldn't keep lying to me, right to my face. If he did that, I could forgive. If he did that, I could help him get better again. If he was honest, I could do anything.

He turned to me slowly, his eyes narrow and his mouth pinched tight. When he opened his mouth, I was sure he was going to admit it. I was sure he was going to come clean. Instead, he said, "No. I'm fine. I'm better. I don't need that shit."

My heart broke into a million pieces. I stood up shakily, my heavy heart thudding against my ribs and echoing in my head. Slowly, I lifted my chin and met his eyes, everything inside of me fracturing into pieces because of what I had to do next. I didn't dare look away from those blue eyes of his I loved so much. "The pharmacy called me. They wanted you to know your prescription was ready."

He froze mid-step. "It's a mistake. I didn't call them in. I swear it. You have to believe me."

Again with the lies. When would it stop? "Finn."

"I swear on my life they're not mine." He came forward and grabbed my hands, squeezing tight. "I'm fine. I'm not in that place again."

Oh, but he was. I might not be his therapist, but I was his wife. And now that my eyes were open, I was seeing so much more. I was seeing it all. The bags under his eyes. The haunted light that never went away. The distraction and the hair pulling.

It was all there.

Nodding, I pulled free and picked up my purse. I took out one, then two, and then three bottles of pills. Two of which were empty. He watched me the whole time, his face growing paler by the second. By the time I plopped down the third, his fists were tight at his sides.

"You lied to me," I said, my voice finally cracking. "Over and over again. Why?"

He covered his face and let out a broken sound. "Shit. I'm sorry. I'm so sorry."

I reached out to hug him, but forced myself to stop. Yes, I loved him. Yes, I wanted to tell him it was okay and kiss him until he felt better. But it wasn't. It really wasn't.

So I said nothing.

chapter
three

Finn

I stared at the pill bottles she'd lined up. My own personal museum of shame, all lined up for the two of us to see. My chest went tight and my breathing got harder with each painful breath. The world was closing in on me, and I was helpless to stop it. Just like before. The voices screaming in my head only got louder, exacerbated by my own internal screaming. They screamed out for help, and so did I.

When I'd gotten injured, the last thing on my mind had been the worry of what might happen. I'd been thinking of bills, and how long I'd have to be off work, and how this would affect my ability to hold Susan for long periods of time. I usually walked her around the house when she was crying, and I'd been worried I wouldn't be able to.

Those had been the thoughts in my head. Not the one I should have been concerned about—whether or not this would be a trigger. I'd thought I was better.

I'd thought I was fixed.

Turns out, all it took was one little fender bender to throw me back into the hell I'd escaped all those years ago, where I'd watched my platoon die all around me. It had been years. Years of nothing except for the occasional nightmare. How was I supposed to know that I should be worried about breaking all over again?

It made me wonder if Carrie had been worried about it. She'd asked me if I'd wanted pills, and I'd said no. She gave me an assessing look and then let it go. I'd been grateful she didn't push it. But then the nightmares had started, and the small spark of fear that I could never shake exploded into an inferno. And the only escape route I found was the same one I'd used all those years ago: the sweet oblivion of the pills.

So I got the prescription filled, hid it from Carrie shamefully, knowing that it could cost me everything I loved. I hadn't cared.

I'd just wanted some peace and quiet so I could live.

What would that life be now?

"Why?" Carrie asked, her voice soft and wrecked. It had been years since I'd heard her this way. So sad. So broken. "Why didn't you come to me?"

"I don't know." I sat down on the couch, my eyes locked on the fireplace. "I thought I'd be okay, I guess."

"Why the pills?"

Anger choked me, and I lashed out at her. I knew I wasn't really angry with her, but I did it anyway. Ugly truth. "Because I thought it would be fun to get high. Why the fuck do you think I took them?"

She flinched. I hated myself right now. "Is your PTSD flaring up?"

She wasn't even acting angry. Why wasn't she yelling at me? Screaming? Hitting me? I deserved it. I deserved it all, and more. I'd let her down again. Let Susan down, too. "Yeah, it is."

"Since the accident?"

I covered my face. "Yes."

"You could have told me."

I lowered my hands and glowered at her. "Yes, because I'm so good at communicating my feelings when it comes to this shit. I'm so open with my failures."

"Having PTSD isn't a *failure*." Finally, she lost that careful, calm expression. She pinched her lips together and stood, hands fisted at her sides. "And don't you dare take that tone with me."

"Oh, sorry," I drawled. "I didn't realize I had to watch my tone around you, *doc*. I mean, if we're going to have a session, I should call you that, right?"

She flushed. "This isn't a session. I'm your wife, not your doctor."

"Funny, it's not feeling that way right now."

A low blow. She'd never once treated me like a patient, not even when we were arguing. Not even when I was being an illogical prick — like right fucking now.

She shook her head. "Don't try to turn the tables on me. That's not fair. I didn't even know you were taking the pills until a few hours ago, and I came home to find you *passed out* with our daughter awake in her playpen. Alone."

I closed my eyes. Never would I have believed I would fall so far. I'd fallen asleep on the job, and there were no excuses for it. I knew it. "I'm sorry."

"What if there had been a fire? Or an earthquake? Or *anything*?" She was turning red, which meant I'd finally gotten her angry. Or maybe she'd been angry all along. "How could you have gotten *high* when you were in charge of her?"

"I don't know!" I shouted.

She jumped. "Please don't yell at me."

I locked gazes with her, dropping the anger I'd been holding on to for dear life. "That's all I hear when I close my eyes. Yelling. Groaning. Sobbing." I tugged on my hair. "Even now, when you're here talking to me? All I hear is them dying, in the back of my mind. They're *dying*, Carrie, right outside our door, and I can't help them. I can't help anyone."

Tears filled her eyes, and she covered her mouth. "Oh my God."

"I just wanted the voices to stop." I closed my eyes. I could see them, as if I was on that field right now, instead of my living room. "There's so much blood. So much death."

She bit down on her lower lip. "Why didn't you tell me?"

"Because I didn't want to." I swallowed past my aching throat, opening my eyes. I was safe in my living room, but I didn't feel safe. Not at all. "Do you want me to leave?"

Part of me wanted her to say yes. She'd be better off without me. The other more selfish part refused to walk away. This was my family. My wife. My entire life.

I couldn't lose them because of a stupid fucking accident.

She crossed her arms, giving me her back. "No. Go back to sleep. You obviously need it. We'll talk more tomorrow when you're sober."

My gut twisted. "Carrie…"

"*No.*" She whirled on me, her face wet with tears. "Don't 'Carrie' me in that voice that makes me want to cry and hug you and forgive you. Just don't."

I held my hands up, a knife twisting in my gut. "Why not?"

"When I came home, I had the horrible fear that you were dead. *Dead*, Finn. Do you have any idea how that feels?" She pressed a hand to her chest. "How much it hurts me that you felt the need to do this, and didn't come to me, your damn wife, for help? *I could have helped you!*"

"I didn't want you to have to!" I shouted, the ever-present rage turning my vision red. So much rage. "I didn't want to be that pitiful guy who you had to nurse back to fucking health again. I didn't want to be a fucking assignment to you. Someone who needed to talk out his fucking pain so he didn't do something irrational and dangerous. So he can maybe actually get some sleep at night, instead of lying there awake, reliving that night over and over again until he starts to doubt his sanity."

"So you'd rather pop pills than admit you need help?" She threw her hands out. "That's the better option than coming to me to talk it out? That's the guy you want to be?"

I gritted my teeth. "Yes. It was."

"I could have sat up with you all night, *every night*, if you needed to talk to someone. If you needed support. I would have skipped meals. Sleep. *Anything*. I could have held you. Loved you. Helped you." She shook her head slowly, tears rolling down her cheeks. "And instead you gave us this. More lies and betrayal."

"That's what I am." I clenched my jaw. "A fucking liar. You knew that already, though. You always had a thing for liars like me. You get off on it."

She backed up, looking as if I'd struck her. I felt as if I had, but the chaos inside me drowned any remorse. "You need help, Finn. You need to talk to someone. And if you won't, in the morning, when you sober up, you need to leave until you figure out if you want to be a part of this family anymore."

No. *No.* This was my home; this was my *family*.

Carrie and Susan were the only things still keeping me sane. I took a step toward her, my heart beating way too fast. Why wouldn't she just *listen* to me? I didn't need help—I just needed *her*. She was my help. She was my *life*. "Carrie—"

"*No.*"

She ran toward the stairs, not saying another word. I let her go, knowing if I followed her, it would only get worse. I'd betrayed her, and she didn't want to be around me. I limped toward the couch, my heart throbbing as badly as my leg. When I sat down, I saw them. She'd left the pills on the table.

Was it a test to see if I could resist temptation?

Or did she just not give a damn anymore?

Two horrible mornings later, I leaned forward on my desk and rubbed my temples, cursing the headache that gathered behind my skull with alarming strength. The codes on my computer screen blurred into an unintelligible blob. I'd gone back to work three days early, against the doctor's advice, because it was better than sitting at the hotel, alone in silence, remembering everything I'd done wrong.

Better than remembering anything at all.

And now I was getting a migraine for my troubles. I didn't get headaches as much as I used to, but they still came. And when they came? They hurt like a fucking bitch.

Guess that's what happens when an IED almost kills you. Everyone else died in the ambush, but this was my booby prize for making it out—skull-crushing headaches.

Even after I'd lived through the blast, I'd wanted to die.

I'd returned home only to lose even more. First my father died, and then I drove Carrie away, unable to manage my demons. It had taken a miracle to get her back, and now I was losing her again, for the same reason. This wasn't supposed to happen again. I was *fixed*. I was fine. But I guess I'd only spackled over the cracks, because here I was again, struggling with an addiction to oblivion.

Losing everything.

Sighing, I looked at the photo on the edge of my desk. Carrie beamed up at me through the glass. She held Susan in her arms. For the last eight years, Carrie had been the shining beacon in my life. I'd been the luckiest man in the world, and I knew it. Thanked my lucky stars about it every day and night.

For eight years, we'd been happy. For eight years, we'd had peace. I guess it was only a matter of time until it all fell apart...and, man, it had.

Because of me. Because I was weak.

I wouldn't be weak anymore.

My phone rang, and I jumped. I'd been expecting it after the text message I'd received earlier, but my PTSD was more than just a collection of waking nightmares. I became battle-ready at every loud noise, and the line between reality and memories was becoming more blurred by the second.

I was drowning all over again, with no one to help me this time, because I'd betrayed the only person who could help me.

The phone rang again, and I stared at it for a second, letting it ring one more time before I moved. Lifting it to my ear, I took a steadying breath like I'd been taught, and said, "Talk to me."

"Finn," said my father-in-law, Senator Wallington.

His voice was even grimmer than it had been when he'd found out I had fallen in love with his baby girl all those years ago. I'd been assigned to protect her, and keep my hands to myself. Instead, I'd fallen in love with her. I'd been out of line, but I hadn't given a damn. I'd loved her too much. But that fear and warning in his voice filled me with dread. I'd been all filled up on bad news lately.

"What's up, Hugh?"

The senator cleared his throat. "We have trouble."

"I gathered as much by your cryptic text earlier," I said drily, closing my eyes. "Explain, please, so I can actually understand what you're trying to say."

"As you know, the bill that would ban guns from all buildings in the state of—"

I stood, impatient to get to the heart of this call as quickly as possible. "Yes. I know. It fell through, because of your vote. We talked about this last month." Before all hell had broken loose. "Some people weren't happy with you."

"Right." A pause, and then, "Well, there's been a threat from an activist. A man named Kyle Farmer."

Well, shit. That wasn't good.

"Do you need me to help you out? Is that why you're calling, sir?" I rubbed my forehead. "I mean, I'd think you'd rather have someone who is still in the business than an almost thirty-two-year-old who doesn't guard anyone anymore and has a limp, but I'm yours if you need me."

Once upon a time, I'd been a Marine *and* a private security guard for Senator Wallington—now my father-in-law. I wasn't really in the mood to go back into security detail, all things considered, but despite everything, he was family.

I didn't really have a choice.

"No, it's worse. Much worse," the senator said.

"How could it be worse than—?" My gut clenched tight. It couldn't be... "No. Don't say it. Carrie? Susan?"

"Apparently this man, this Kyle Farmer guy, he lost his daughter to violence. Gun violence." Hugh paused. "I received photos in the mail. Photos of Carrie going to work. Carrying Susan into daycare. Out on a date with you."

I closed my eyes, the voices getting louder. Drowning him out. "Son of a bitch."

"It says he's going to take what I took from him—my daughter's life." Senator Wallington took a deep breath. "An eye for an eye, he says."

My fingers tightened over the phone. It had been years since we had to worry about Carrie's safety. *Years.* Now this? Fucking shit.

It couldn't have come at a worst time.

The senator continued without a reply from me, which was good, because I didn't think I could talk right now. "I know you're not her guard anymore, and haven't been for years. I know she doesn't need one, or didn't, but we need to—"

"He won't get near her." I sank into my chair. "I won't let him anywhere near her, I swear it. I'll be at her side twenty-four seven." *Whether or not she likes it,* I added silently. I glanced over my shoulder at the clock. Almost five. She'd be heading home soon, so I'd have to hurry if I wanted to beat her there. "Who else will you be sending out?"

"No one. Just you."

I stopped mid-reach for my keys. I narrowed my eyes. I smelled bullshit, right up in my face. "What?"

"You're all she needs." He cleared his throat. "And I want you to send Susan here to me."

Okay, that made absolutely no fucking sense. "My daughter?" I blinked. "Hell no. She's safer with me."

"Not if you're with Carrie. Carrie is the target, so we need to split them up."

"Bullshit, Hugh." I sank back against the chair. "Tell me the real reason you want Susan for the weekend. What's up?"

He spluttered. "I don't know what—"

"*Hugh.*"

"Fine." He sighed impatiently. "How did you know?"

"You'd never send the two of us away alone if you thought there was a true threat to her," I said, studying my nails. "You'd have the whole fucking army on her."

"True." He made an annoyed sound. "I should have known better."

I tapped my foot impatiently. "What's really up, Hugh?"

"The guy I told you about is real. He did make a threat."

"Is he something to be worried about?" I asked, sitting straighter.

"I doubt it," he admitted. "But it's a threat nonetheless."

"Why send us away alone, then?"

"Because he's not a *huge* threat," Hugh said, sighing. "And you two are falling apart. She didn't tell me anything, but I've been married a long time, and I know how to recognize a rough patch when I see one. You two need a romantic weekend alone."

I collapsed against the chair, closing my eyes. "How much do you know?"

"Enough." He hesitated. "I know you two need to get away to talk."

I rubbed my forehead. "I don't know."

"If we tell her about the threat, and make it sound worse than it is, she'll agree to go away with you."

"No." I opened my eyes, my grip on the phone painfully tight. "No more lies. If you want to show up and tell her that you're sending us away for the weekend, then fine. Tell her that. But don't blow up a threat if it's not one."

"It *is*." He sighed. "But we'll get him, I'm sure. He's no crazier than any other nutjob who's written me hate mail, I'd dare to say."

"Then don't mention the threat at all."

"Fine. I'm on my way to your house now. I'll be there in an hour or so. When I get there, we'll tell her that I wanted a weekend with my baby girl, and I'm sending you two to a cabin in the woods for some relaxation. It's a Christmas present." A voice sounded in the background, and the senator's muffled reply came through. "I need to go. Don't tell her I called you before coming over."

The phone clicked off, and I sat there with it in my hand for so long, the dial tone sounded. Jerking back to life, I set it down on the receiver. Pushing my chair back, I stood and grabbed my keys off the desk. It might not be easy, but I had to find a way to get her to go to that cabin with me. I had to find a way to get her alone so we could talk.

It was time to hash it all out. Time to find out if she wanted me to leave for good, or if she wanted to keep fighting for what we'd once had. Only she could answer that.

I got in my truck and started the familiar ride home. The one I hadn't taken in two days. As I turned down the windy road that led to home, our neighbor, Mrs. Easton, waved at me with a big smile. She probably thought I'd been away for work, since I hadn't been home. No one knew why I'd left.

I waved back and forced a smile, even though I felt more like snarling than anything else. When I pulled into my driveway, I scanned the bushes. No one seemed to be lurking in the shadows, waiting to kill my wife. Sure, the threat might not be huge, but it was a threat nonetheless. And I'd keep my eyes open.

I killed the ignition and got out of the car. Dragging my hands through my hair, I made my way around the home we'd built together. There was no one here. No one at all.

Slowly, I lowered myself to the first step on the porch. I could go inside, but I sat down instead. It was easier to watch for incoming traffic this way. Headlights came down the road almost instantly. I recognized the Mercedes right away.

Carrie was home.

My heart sped up painfully, and I stood up awkwardly. Shoving my hands into my pockets, I held my breath. Would she still come home, or would she drive past me in an attempt to avoid the conversation we'd both been trying to ignore? She slowed down to a crawl, her blue eyes locked on me through the tinted windshield.

Then, slowly, she pulled into the driveway next to my truck. Her car shut off, and I swallowed hard. I limped toward her car, but each step felt harder than the last.

Would she tell me to leave again?

I opened her car door for her, and she didn't look at me. Just stared straight ahead, her hands tight on the wheel. "Finn."

So much was said with that one word. So fucking much.

"I...I wanted to see Susan." *And you. I miss you.* I moved away from her door. My heart twisted at the sight of her tight expression. She looked haunted. So distant. *Empty.* "She's my daughter, too, Carrie."

"I know that. You can see her whenever you want, of course." She tightened her grip on the wheel, but her voice was even tighter. She sounded as if she was wound so taut, she just might snap if pushed any further. And it was my fault. "You can get her out of the car, if you'd like."

"Thank you."

I opened the door and peeked in at the rear-facing car seat. My precious baby girl was already thirteen months, and I couldn't believe time had passed so fast. When she saw me, she squealed and gurgled, a bright smile lighting up her face.

Her lower jaw was covered in a shiny sheen of drool. "*Dah-dah!*"

"Yeah, it's me." Despite the turmoil inside of me, I couldn't help but grin back. It was probably the first time I'd smiled in two days. I needed her in my life. "Hey, baby girl."

"Gah!" She flailed her fists excitedly, smacking me in the eye. "Dah-dah!"

My heart didn't twist. It fucking broke. "It's me." I wiped my hand over her face, drying her off so she didn't get a rash. "I missed you, baby girl. Did you miss me?"

She smiled at me and caught my hand.

I took that as a yes.

Carrie made a broken sound, and dropped her head against the headrest on her driver's seat. I stared at the back of the head I knew so well, wanting to say something to fix this, but unable to come up with a single fucking word to do so. Believe me. I'd tried.

"Can I come in?" I asked, hating the way my voice cracked.

"Yes," Carrie said, her voice perfectly flat and even. "You can come in. We need to talk, anyway."

I undid Susan's latch. Even though I knew this, a part of me didn't want to talk. If we talked, she might tell me she was done with me for good. And if she was done with me, then I wouldn't know what to do with myself.

But instead of saying all that, I settled for: "Yeah. We do."

As I followed her inside, clutching a squirming Susan tight to my chest, I scanned the yard again. No one was there. She was still safe.

But I wasn't.

chapter
four

Carrie

As I walked up to the door, I tried not to turn around and glance at Finn. I wanted to run into his arms and hug him and beg him never to leave us again. And I wanted to kiss him until I ran out of breath, and then kiss him some more. I wanted to hit him for doing what he did, and I wanted to kill him. But mostly, I wanted to love him.

I wanted to love him so badly.

But I *already* loved him more than life itself, and that's what made this so hard. He was the man who'd carried my heart in his hands for so long, and still did, even if he didn't realize it. If he did, he wouldn't have done what he did. He wouldn't have broken my trust like he did, over and over again throughout the years.

I'd forgiven him instantly so many times, for so many things, but this last time had been the last straw. Silently, I pressed a hand to my stomach again. We had a little family now. I needed to think of that before I thought of my own wants and desires. No matter how much it hurt.

Even if I felt like I was slowly dying without him in my life.

Calmly, I undid the lock on the front door. It had taken us three weeks to finally agree on this door. He'd wanted red. I'd wanted blue. We'd settled on green. Then we'd made love for an hour after we bought it, happy as could be that we were finally getting our dream home. Now we had nothing.

Finn's refusal to get help was putting a strain on everything, and it just might be the end of us, too. I tried to act as if it didn't rip my heart apart to see him again; after all we'd been through. Especially since he kept giving me that Finn-look that always made me melt. The same one that had gotten him his way in pretty much everything for the past eight years of our lives.

Opening the door, I turned on the security code and let him walk in first. He limped forward, Susan held securely in his arms. It was on the tip of my tongue to ask him if he was okay, if he needed anything from me, but I bit the words back.

I stayed silent. I had no idea how, but I did.

The other night after we'd fought, I'd left the pills on the table. When I'd woken up in the morning, he'd been gone. So had the pills. Had he taken them all?

Or was he trying to get better?

If he was trying, I could help him. I wanted to help him. But only if he wanted it. Only if he was ready. I couldn't force him. He had to decide it all on his own.

I looked at him again. He wore the dark gray suit I loved. I'd gotten it for him last year, and I'd also painstakingly searched for a blue shirt to match his eyes. It had taken forever, but I had finally found one. He'd made love to me for hours to make up for the hours I'd spent looking for the shirt.

God, this hurt so much.

He kissed Susan's temple, his eyes focused on me. He had a bit of a five o'clock shadow going on. I loved it when he was stubbly, and he knew it. Maybe he'd grown it on purpose. Just to torture me. If so, it was working. I wanted nothing more than to throw myself in his arms and never let go again. I missed him so much.

So, so much.

But I forced myself to stiffen up, and straightened to my full height. "How are you feeling?"

"I'm all better."

The fact that he truly believed that broke my heart, too. He wasn't all better. Not at all. "The pills." I took a deep breath. "Did you take them at the proper times?"

He kissed Susan again, and shook his head. "No. I haven't taken them at all. I flushed them all at my hotel. I slipped up, Ginger. It was only a couple of days, really. I haven't had any more. I swear it. I'm good now."

I wanted to believe him, but I wasn't so sure I did. Too many lies.

Too many secrets. Too many times. "Okay."

"Do you believe me?"

I hugged myself and looked at the clock, refusing to answer that. "I'm going to go start dinner for her."

He glanced away. "Right. Of course."

I headed into the kitchen, feeling as if he had a grip on my heart, and he was ripping it out of my chest one painful yank at a time. This isn't how we were supposed to be acting right before Thanksgiving. We were supposed to be baking pies and talking about decorating our tree, just like we had been for years.

Not this. Anything but *this*.

"Carrie," he said, following me into the kitchen. "Can't you just give me—"

I gripped the edge of the counter tight. "I don't want to talk about this yet. Not in front of her." I spun on him, heart racing. "You...you..."

Broke my heart. My trust. Everything.

Could have hurt our child.

He swallowed. "I know. Believe me, I know. But we swore to love each other forever, Ginger. For better or worse."

Ginger. His nickname for me.

"I know." I gripped the cold granite edge even tighter. "But it's not just us anymore. It's her too. It's... What if...?" I closed my eyes, shutting my mind off. "She was with you, Finn. And you were high. Passed out on the couch."

He glanced away, his jaw hard. "But I stopped the pills. I'm fine now."

"It scares me that you think that," I said, my tone cajoling. "What if you hurt Susan? What if you drove with her, thinking you were okay, and you crashed?"

"Jesus, Carrie. I'd *never* have done that. And I never will." He hugged Susan even closer. She yanked on his ear, and he flinched. I didn't know if it was from that or my words, but he did. "High or sober. Weak or strong. I'd never, ever endanger you two."

I pressed a hand to my stomach. It roiled in response to the horrible images of them lying dead in a ditch. They'd been haunting me ever since I found him on the couch. "So you were going to have the pills delivered, or what? Because if you weren't, you would have driven with her."

He paled. "Not high."

"But you *were* high. And you *did*. You weren't home all those days."

"I made a mistake." His voice cracked on the last word. It broke my heart even more. "I'm sorry. So fu—freaking sorry."

"Yeah, I know that. You always are, and I always forgive you, but that doesn't make it okay." Nothing was okay anymore. Nothing at all. My heart yanked out another fraction of an inch, and I gave him my back. "Go play with Susan. I'll cook her dinner."

I thought he might argue with me, but he headed through the kitchen, making his way toward the living room. As I reached out for the pot, I knocked the lid and an open box of pasta on the floor. The lid hit the linoleum with a loud clash, while the pasta spilled all over the place, and Finn leapt back, his face ashen and sweat covering his forehead almost immediately. I hadn't realized he'd come back in.

"No," he whispered. "Not again."

"No one's here," I said slowly, keeping my voice monotone. "I just dropped the pot lid."

He hugged Susan close to his chest, his hand splayed protectively over her small head, and his eyes darted back and forth, looking for the threat. He looked terrified.

I forced myself to stand still, letting him process the fear. After a few seconds, he locked eyes on me, visibly relaxing after a few deep breaths. More than likely, he was counting them in his head. I let him. "You okay?" he asked.

"Yes." I pressed a hand to my heart, watching him closely. If I'd needed any confirmation that he'd slipped back into the deep abyss of PTSD, I'd gotten it. He needed help, *real* help from a professional, and I couldn't be the one to give it to him. "Are you?"

He nodded once. "Yeah. You just caught me off guard, is all." He glanced at me, his expression guarded. He must've seen the concern in mine. "I'm okay."

"I know." I kept my tone light and tender. "Are you sleeping?"

He tightened his lips. "You're not my therapist. If you want to know how I'm sleeping, let me come back home."

"Go on and play with Susan," I said, ignoring the giant elephant in the room with PTSD stamped on its forehead. If I pushed him too hard, I'd only make him more defensive. I had to approach this carefully. "I'll pick this mess up on my own."

He gave me one last look, opened his mouth, and closed it again before leaving the room as I asked. After cleaning up and filling the pot with water, I covered my face and tried to think of a way to help him. A way he'd accept my help. In the distance, I could hear him talking to Susan in that soft voice that he reserved for only her.

She made a cute sound, and Finn laughed again. The whole scene sounded so normal that I almost forgot what had happened.

When the doorbell rang, I jumped even higher than Finn had earlier. I glanced at the clock. Who the heck would be here now? I hadn't been expecting anyone. Finn came into the kitchen at an almost-run, Susan clutched in his arms.

He didn't look scared this time, but he looked determined. "Your dad's here."

"No." I pulled the curtains back. Sure enough, it was my dad. "*No*. Why would he come here unannounced like this? Did you tell him about us?"

He tugged on one of his curls. "No. Of course not."

"Well, then, why is he here?" I hissed.

He quirked a light brown brow, his blue eyes I loved so much locked on me. "Open the door and find out."

I stared at him, and took a deep breath. As I exhaled, I undid the lock. "Act normal. As if nothing happened. He can't know about us."

"Yep." Finn nodded once. "I'll be normal."

After one more calming breath, I opened the door. "Dad! What a surprise!"

Dad grinned at me, and within seconds he'd picked me up and was hugging me, like he used to do when I was a girl. His arms closed around me, and his familiar scent of Old Spice and coconut shampoo washed over me.

The desire to collapse in his arms and cry was overbearing, but I held it together. He didn't need to know everything was falling apart. He couldn't know. It was between my husband and me. No one else.

"Hey, Princess." He kissed my forehead, cradling the back of my head with his hand. "I missed you."

"Come in," Finn said, clearing his throat and stepping forward. With a flick of his wrist, he closed the door behind my dad. "It's nice seeing you, sir."

"Back at you." Dad let go of me, and offered Finn his hand. "How are things going?"

Finn shook his hand. "Wonderful."

He glanced at me out of the corner of his eye and put his arm around my shoulders. He was trying to act normal, but it made my chest get all tight and I couldn't breathe. All I could smell was his woodsy Dolce and Gabbana cologne.

God, I missed him. Missed his touch. His smell. His skin.

"Just having a quiet night at home with the family," Finn said, squeezing my shoulders.

I forced a smile. It probably looked demented.

Dad nodded. "Excellent."

"What made you come all the way out here?" I asked, trying to keep my voice light when I felt like I was about to break. "You and Mom get in another fight over curtains?"

They'd just bought a vacation house out here in Cali, to be close to us. Decorating it had been tough, to say the least. "Ha! Nope. Just wanted to drop by and see how you guys were doing."

"Oh." I nodded, feeling like a freaking bobblehead. "I see."

"You sound unhappy I'm here." Dad studied me, his eyes narrowed in the way he always did when suspicious of something. "Everything okay?"

"Yes. God, yes. Everything is great. Fabulous. Wonderful. Superb. Fanta—"

Finn cleared his throat. "I think he gets it, Ginger." He squeezed my shoulders, silently telling me to play it cool, which I obviously wasn't. "One more adjective isn't necessary," he said lightly.

"Right." I forced a smile. "What's up, Dad?"

He stared at us, not talking. I knew that *he* knew we were acting strangely, but hopefully he didn't push the issue. "I brought you an early Christmas present. I'm taking Susan home with me tonight."

I blinked at him. "You want to take her away? Why?"

Finn stayed silent.

"I'm sending you and your husband away for a romantic weekend for two. Just you, Finn, and the woods." He smiled and snatched Susan out of Finn's arms. "I remember after we had you, your mother and I did the same thing. We needed some alone time after the exhaustion of raising a baby."

"What?" I shook my head, panic rising in my throat. "No. We can't. I mean...we can't. *No*. No way."

Dad raised his brows. "Why not?"

"Because I..." I glanced at Finn, silently asking for help. He stared back at me silently, completely unhelpful. "I just can't let Susan go without a moment's notice like that. And I can't leave right now. Work is too busy."

"You can make it work. It's the weekend. And if you need money, you can always ask me for some help. You know that." Dad crossed his arms. "Unless there's something you're not telling me?"

Finn shifted his feet and tugged on his hair again. "I'll go pack up some clothes for Susan. Thank you for your kind present, sir. We appreciate it."

Dad nodded once. "You're welcome."

Finn went upstairs, and I collapsed on the bottom step. "Dad, this wasn't expected at all."

"That's the point of a surprise. It's *supposed* to be unexpected."

"Oh, believe me, it was," I muttered under my breath.

But now that I'd overcome the initial panic at the idea of an intimate weekend away with Finn, maybe this wasn't such a bad idea after all. It might be the perfect opportunity for me to find out just how deep Finn had fallen again.

It might give me a chance to help him come back, and it might be the perfect opportunity to get him to see that he needed help. He had to see it for himself.

Just like last time.

"Carrie?" Dad asked, waving his hand in my face. "You in there?"

I snapped out of it. "Uh, yeah. I'm excited, that's all. Thanks, Dad." I stood up and kissed his cheek, then rubbed Susan's hair off her cheek for her. "We needed a weekend away."

Dad smiled. "I'm happy to help. Your mother is, too."

"Why didn't she come with you?" I asked.

"She's shopping for Susan's arrival." Dad rolled his eyes. "You know how she is."

"I'm going to have to build a new closet for her, aren't I?"

Dad laughed.

Finn came down the stairs, small luggage bag in his hand. "All packed."

"That quick?" I looked at the bag. It seemed awfully light. "Are there enough clothes in there?"

"With your mother shopping as we speak?" Finn shrugged. "We should be good."

"The man has a point." Dad took the bag and slung it over his shoulder. "I already have a car seat, so we'll be out of the way now. Say goodbye."

"But I was cooking her dinner!" I said quickly. "Stay for a little while and—"

"I have a meal waiting for her at home. Chef made her favorite." Dad pulled an envelope out of his jacket pocket and handed it off to Finn, but his eyes never left mine. "Here are the keys. You two need to get started on that romantic weekend. If you head out now, you can make it there by nine. The cabin will be stocked with everything you need. Wine. Food. Firewood. The two of you can stay inside, and not have to leave at all the whole time. Ignore the world and all your troubles."

If only it was so easy.

chapter
five

Finn

I followed Carrie up the well-worn path to the cabin, holding our bags in my hands. I couldn't believe how easily she agreed to her father's plan, quite honestly. I'd expected her to agree to go, but not *actually* go. I'd expected a fight from her.

Instead, she'd just started packing her bags.

Glancing over at Carrie, I studied her profile. She unlocked the door and pushed it open. After she flicked the light on, she blinked against the brightness and tugged off her green fingerless mittens. I still remembered her knitting them, right before the accident.

Before all hell had broken loose.

She glanced around the cabin and headed straight for the kitchen without a word to me. I didn't follow her. Instead, I checked out the security of the cabin with a critical eye. Just in case the idle threat became an *un*-idle one.

There were only three windows, from what I could see, and one entry, so her father had chosen a smart location for defense. The cabin might look small and quaint on the outside, but on the inside it was more luxurious than cozy. Leather couches, maple wood tables, and glass lamps filled the living room, which had a huge glass fireplace in the center.

The kitchen beyond the living room was all granite countertops and maple cabinets. It had an island too. The whole cabin smelled like apple cinnamon. The room leading to the left must be the bedroom, so I headed that way with the bags. I turned on the light with my elbow, and froze. A red velvet comforter topped the king-size bed, and there was a hot tub in the corner of the room.

A fucking hot tub *in* the bedroom.

In another lifetime, before I'd fucked it all up, we'd have had a lot of fun in this room. Now, I'd probably be on the couch, and she'd be in here alone. Sometimes I hated myself. Sometimes I hated her a little bit, too.

Not as much as I loved her, of course, but enough that it tasted bad.

She'd sworn to love me forever, for better or for worse. I'd been great for years. I'd been a clean, sober, supportive, loving husband and father. But the second I slipped up, she was done with me. She told me I should leave.

That wasn't what love was supposed to be, was it?

Shit if I knew anymore. Rubbing my jaw, I tossed the bags on the bed. I might not know much, but I knew one thing—if I was looking for the perfect chance to remind her just how good we fit together? This. Was. It.

We were in a cabin together in the middle of fucking nowhere. She had nowhere to go. All she needed was a reminder of how much we loved each other, and everything could go back to normal. We'd be back to being *us*, and I could go home.

I shut the bedroom light off and walked into the living room, but I only made it two steps before I froze. Carrie popped a cork, and the sudden sound sent a shaft of fear racing through my veins. I staggered back, my hand reaching for the gun I'd started wearing again. Wearing it made me feel safer in a world of mayhem, craziness, and unpredictability.

Before I withdrew it from the holster, though, I pulled my shit together. I held off the panic with a deep, calming breath. She dumped the champagne down the kitchen sink and clunked it on the counter loudly. Then she picked up another one and struggled with the bottle of Asti. She hadn't seen me yet, and had missed my mini freak-out. Thank fucking God.

Shoving my hands in my pockets, I came closer. I tried my best to look cool and calm. Collected and in control. Everything I was not. "Are you sure you want to do that? You're stuck here with me all weekend. You might need to drink to survive."

"Yes, I'm sure." She struggled to pop the cork, not looking my way. "We don't need this in here with us."

In other words, she didn't want me to slip and get drunk, as well as getting high. She didn't need to worry. I had no interest in any of that shit, but she'd never believe me. Not after what I'd done. "Let me help you."

She finally looked at me. "It's okay," she said softly. "I can do it."

"I assure you I can touch a fucking bottle without turning into a slurring drunk," I snapped, stalking across the room and coming up behind her. "Let me help."

Reaching over her shoulder, I gently pried her fingers off the bottle. She hesitated, but finally let go. "Okay."

"I'm not drinking, and I'm not taking pills," I repeated. "I'm better now."

She opened her mouth, closed it, and pushed off the counter. When she reached the corner of the kitchen, as far away from me as she could get without leaving the room, she crossed her arms and watched me. "Have you thought about getting help again? Dr. Montgomery helped you so much last time."

"I don't need her this time." I popped the cork. "I'm not as bad as I was when we were younger. I'm fine, Ginger. Really."

She wrung her hands. "Finn..."

I shrugged. "Don't worry. You'll see it for yourself when we're here. You'll see I'm good again. I don't want pills or drinks or anything. I only want you," I said.

So fucking badly it hurt.

"Are you sleeping yet?"

She'd asked me that earlier. I'd avoided the answer because I wasn't. If she knew that, she'd have another reason to keep me away. If she knew how dark I was right now, she'd never trust me again. Especially if she knew how unbalanced I was right now.

The thoughts in my head sobered me.

If I was this messed up, maybe I shouldn't be trying to get her to let me back in. Maybe it was better this way, with her in our house, and me in a hotel. Maybe I shouldn't be around people right now. Maybe she was safer without me. Maybe they all were.

Shitfuckdamn. How had I let myself fall so far, so fast?

But I could fix it. I was already getting better. I just—

She cleared her throat. "Are you going to answer me?"

I snapped back to attention. "No. I'm not sleeping. I'm not sleeping at all." I stared down at the bottle in my hand, anger and frustration hitting me hard. "Maybe that's because I'm in a crappy hotel bed instead of at home where I belong, though." As soon as I said it, I wanted to punch myself in the nuts for making it seem as if it was her fault I was a fucked-up mess. That wasn't fair, and I knew it. "Carrie...I..."

She crossed her arms. She looked so strong. I wished I were half as strong as she was right now. "You're the one who hid your symptoms from me. You're the one who made it quite clear that you didn't want to involve me in this."

I shrugged. "I don't want to be your pet project or your live-in patient."

"I don't have to be involved in all aspects of it, but I have a right, as your wife, to know if there's something wrong. I don't think it's wrong of me to expect that." She held her hands out. "But you *do* need help."

You need help. Those were fast becoming my three most hated words in the whole fucking universe. I'd thought I'd been done hearing those words after all those years, but she couldn't see that I wasn't the same guy I'd been back then. I could get better on my own.

Already I'd stopped with the pills. The rest would follow. Sure, the nightmares were still there, as was the fear, but I was used to that. I'd already been living with it for years. All of that would calm down eventually.

I just needed to come home.

"*No.*"

"Okay." She let it drop. She would, because as a therapist, she'd know to tread lightly. Not to push me too hard. I knew all their tricks. She bit her lip. "We need to discuss sleeping arrangements."

"I'll take the couch." I slid the empty bottle across the counter and reached for the next one. "Jesus, did your dad think we were going to throw a fucking rave, or what?"

"Apparently," she said drily.

Her lips had twitched for a brief second, but then she'd tamped it down. As if she was scared to actually smile in front of me. As if she was worried if she smiled, I might forget that I'd let her down. Didn't she realize that wasn't something I'd ever forget? I fell asleep thinking about it, and it was the first thing on my mind when I woke up.

How much I'd fucked up again.

"Or he was hoping for a second grandchild," I said, easily popping the cork on the bottle in my hands. "Too bad he won't be getting that now. Not from me anyway."

She bit down on her lower lip again. "Is that your way of saying you're leaving me for good?"

I was leaving *her*? Was she fucking insane? She'd told me to get out. Not the other way around. "I thought *you* made it pretty clear you were done with me when you told me to get out of our home."

"I was scared," she whispered. "You scared me. You're scaring me now, as well."

My heart twisted. I'd never wanted to do that. Never that.

29

But truth be told? I was scaring myself, too.

"Yeah." I stared down at the empty sink. "I know."

She threaded her fingers together in front of her stomach. "Let me ask you this. What do you want from me?"

I wanted her to forget all about what had happened. I wanted her to love me again. I wanted her to stop reminding me how fucked up I was, and hug me close. Tell me I'd be okay. Tell me we'd be okay. But that wasn't going to happen, because I wasn't.

And neither were we.

"I don't know." I dumped the bottle, watching the pale liquid go down the drain. "But I never said I was done with you. I swore to love you forever, and I will. Whether you love me, hate me, or don't give a shit about me, one way or the other, I'll love you."

"I'd never hate you." She shook her head, backing away a step. "You know that."

"You might not hate me, but I think you're done with me."

"Obviously not, or I wouldn't be here," she said, her cheeks flushing with anger.

"Or you're just not ready to admit it yet. You'll have to eventually say it, Ginger." I slid the bottle across the counter and grabbed the last one harshly. "It's easy. Just say, 'I don't want to be with you anymore, Finn. We're done.'"

She'd be better off without me.

She shook her head even faster. "I'm not. We're not. Susan needs her father, and I need my husband, but that man is not who you are right now. You're drowning. And all you need is a little help finding your way back to dry land, if you'd just let yourself take it. If you'd just take what you want and turn it into—"

I set the bottle down on the counter harder than necessary. She jumped. "I know what I want. I want you."

She closed her eyes, not saying anything.

What was there to say? I wanted her, and she wanted me gone. Our story was over. "Would it be easier for you to say it if I became a total asshole again?"

"W-What?"

I stared at her, bottle in hand. "I could drink this in front of you, like I did the last time we broke up. I could act like I don't give a shit about you or us or Susan. I could tell you a bunch of bullshit lies again, so you get pissed off at me all over again. Then you could justify it. Then you could make it easier on yourself. Is that what you want?"

"No. Of course not, you fucking idiot." She balled her fists at her sides. She was cursing. That meant she was pissed. Good. I was pissed too. "If I wanted to get rid of you, do you think I would be here with you now?"

My heart sped up. Fucking stupid heart, always putting hope where hope didn't belong. "Does that mean you want to keep me?"

She stared at me silently, as strong as ever. I'd always admired that about her. I'd spent my life protecting her, but she didn't need it. Not really. She could take care of herself. She didn't need me. Not like I needed her. "It means I'm confused, and hurt, and lost," she said.

"I know what it feels like to be lost." I undid the twist lid on the last bottle of wine and dumped it. "I always have been lost without you, but you knew that already."

We locked eyes, and for the first time since she kicked me out, I felt like she actually *saw* me. But then the motion detector light outside lit up and ruined it all. The screams in my head got louder, as if they sensed the risk before I did and were trying to warn me of the impending danger.

Eyes narrowed, I walked past her. "Stay here. Don't move."

"Finn?" she asked, her voice soft. "What's up?"

"Just stay here, and don't follow me," I snapped, heading for the door. "Ask questions later."

I glanced over my shoulder. After a second's hesitation, she moved away from the window behind her with wide eyes. I pushed the curtain back just enough to see what was outside. A deer chewed grass on the front lawn, completely oblivious to the tension he'd brought out in me. I stood there, watching for any other signs of movement.

The deer took off after a few seconds, and nothing followed it. Not even a fucking bunny hopped out of the bushes. Still, I watched. After a tense minute, I sighed and the light turned off. I stood there, making sure it didn't come back on.

"Finn?"

"It's safe. It's just a deer," I murmured, glancing over my shoulder at her. "Nothing's out there."

She pressed her lips together, her pale face framed by her wavy red hair. She came up to me, stopping directly behind me. So close I could smell her perfume and shampoo. So close I wanted nothing more than to hold her close and kiss her until she remembered how good we were together. Until she needed me again.

Her eyes were locked on my hand. "When did you start carrying that again?"

"What?" I looked down and froze. I'd pulled my gun out and hadn't even realized it. "Oh. Recently."

She reached out with a shaking hand, closing her fingers around mine. "Can I have it? Please?"

"What?" My fingers tightened. "Why?"

"Because I love you." She looked up at me, her eyes melancholy. "And you shouldn't have this when you're battling such a dark time in your life. If you…if you hurt yourself…it would kill me. I'd die, too, Finn. Please give me the gun."

My stomach tightened as if I'd been sucker-punched. She thought I was suicidal again? Did she think I was that far gone? Hell, *was* I? I wasn't so sure anymore.

What was wrong with me?

"I'm not going to do that." I gripped the gun tighter, refusing to let go. "I wouldn't do something like that to you and Susan."

She nodded solemnly. "I know. But you drew your weapon without even knowing it. What if I made a sound behind you and scared you? What if you acted without thinking, and something happened?"

I would never intentionally hurt her, but she had a point. What if I unintentionally hurt her? I didn't think that would happen, but was I willing to gamble her life on it? Still, I hesitated. "I can just put it in my luggage so I can get to it if I need to."

She licked her lips, her eyes locked on mine. "I'd feel better if I knew it was gone, and if I knew where it was. For my own peace of mind, please?"

"Don't analyze me like one of your patients," I said, my jaw tight. "I'm not them."

"I know, and I wouldn't." She held a hand over her heart. "I swear this is me, your *wife*, talking. Not the therapist. I wouldn't bring that here. I don't bring my work home with me, and you know it. Please, just give me the gun."

I hesitated. It was as if I was admitting I had a problem if I gave it to her. I didn't, I was fine. I had to be fine. "Carrie…"

"Please?"

I closed my eyes and let go, trying to show her I was trusting her. That I wasn't pushing her away, like I had before. She took the gun and walked away. By the time she came back, I'd pulled my shit together. I felt in control again.

If such a thing existed in my life anymore.

"Why did you pull your gun out?" she asked. "Is something wrong? Is there something you're not telling me?"

"Remember when we first met?" I opened my eyes and looked at her. She watched me closely, not backing off. "Remember that night on the beach? You were escaping a party—"

"And I found you." She hugged herself. "Yeah. Of course I remember. It was the night that started the rest of my life."

Mine too. "Do you remember what I said to you?"

"Every word." She cocked her head inquisitively. I loved it when

32

she did that. It was adorable. "Can you be a little more specific?"

"I told you I was a Marine, and it was my job to protect people." I shrugged. "That hasn't changed. I might not be a Marine anymore, but I'll never stop guarding you. Protecting you. Loving you. But I think you've stopped loving me."

Her bright blue eyes widened, and she shook her head. "You're wrong. I could never stop. But you're hurting, Finn. I can see it. This feeling that you're in control and no one needs to help you?" She rested her hands on my chest, and my heart sped up. "It's false. You need help. You need support. And you need love. I can be two of those things to you, but not three."

But I didn't need another therapist in my life to get better. What I needed was *her*. If I had her again, I could get better. If I had her, then nothing would stand in my way. If I got back in her arms, she'd see I was better. She'd *make* me better.

And I knew I would stop at nothing to get there again. Nothing at all. "I know."

"And you—" She broke off, blinking up at me in surprise. "Wait, what?"

"I know I need help." And *she* would give it to me. Her, and no one else. If I went to a therapist again, I'd be admitting I was weak. I'd been so strong for so long, and I refused to let a stupid fucking car accident break me down. "You're right. I'll get it."

I pulled her closer. She let me, because she believed my words. The tension between us was so thick I could slash it with a knife. I lowered my gaze to her luscious pink mouth. My entire body screamed at me to kiss her. To take away our worries and pain with a gesture so familiar to me that I could do it in my sleep.

"I'm so happy to hear that," she said. "I think you'll feel so much better after you go back to Dr. Montgomery."

I didn't correct her and tell her that I had no intention of seeing that doctor again. I'd said I needed to get help, and I would. But not like that. I lowered my face to hers. I knew what I needed to feel better, and it was right here. Tugging on a strand of her long red hair, I asked, "Can I come home?"

"I never said you couldn't," she breathed, her grip tightening on me. "If you're ready to get help, to keep me in the loop, then yes. You can come home."

"I will. I swear it." I lowered my face even more. "I need you so damn bad. Let me kiss you. Let me make it better. I know how to make it all better."

I brushed my lips across hers gently, testing her reaction. She kissed me back. So soft I barely felt it, and yet I somehow felt it down to my soul.

With a small groan, I closed my mouth over hers, crushing her against my chest and holding her so tightly I might have broken a rib. Man, I'd been waiting for this moment. For her to stop shutting me out. For her to want me as much as I needed her.

And now it was happening.

I slanted my mouth over hers, taking full control of the kiss. Backing her up against the wall, my tongue glided inside her mouth at the same time I slipped my leg in between hers. She gasped and opened her mouth wider, granting me full access.

Without hesitation, I took it, and then I took some more.

Like the greedy asshole I really was.

Part of me knew I should stop kissing her until I was better, but the other part of me wanted her too damn badly to give a shit about anything else. When I closed my hands around her hips, my fingers digging into the soft sides of her ass, she broke off the kiss and took a shaky breath.

I latched onto her neck, biting with just enough pressure to sting. It had been too long since I'd had her. Too long since I'd held her. Too long for everything. My injured leg protested against the weight I put on it, but I ignored the cry of protest it gave.

Any pain I had to suffer was worth it, as long as Carrie was in my arms again, making those small sounds that drove me fucking insane.

"I need you." I hauled her leg up around my waist, pressing my cock against her hot pussy. "I need you naked, screaming, and crying out my name. *Now*."

She nodded. "I love you. I love you so much," she whispered, kissing me again.

And just like that, the guilt hit me. I'd promised to go to a therapist when I had no intention of following through with that promise. I was lying to her again.

What the fuck was wrong with me?

I pulled back, letting out a shattered breath. "Shit."

"What?" She looked up at me, her eyes wide. "What's wrong?"

"We, uh, we need to slow down." I rested my forehead on hers. "I don't want to rush this." *Don't want to hurt you again.* I let go of her, even though it physically hurt to do so, letting out a ragged breath. "We said a lot tonight. Did a lot. Maybe it's time to take a step back."

She nodded. "Of course. You're right."

"See? I paid attention at all those sessions eight years ago." I tugged on my hair, staring back at her. "I know when I need to pull back. When I need to stop. I don't need to go back for her to tell me the same stuff. I'm fine."

"You might think that's true," she said, her eyes locked on mine. "And you're saying all the right things, but now I can't believe them."

"Because I lied to you," I said lifelessly. It always came back to lies I'd told. All the fucking lies. "Again."

She nodded once, pressing a hand to her heart. "I understand you're suffering, and I know it hurts, but you know how important honesty is to me, and yet you lied anyway. No matter your reasons, that *hurts*. It hurts a lot. And the fact that you refuse to admit you could benefit from help…that hurts, too."

"I'm sorry." I tried to keep my voice as even as I could manage under the circumstances. Taking a step closer, I pulled her into my arms and hugged her. She let me. I rested my cheek on top of her head, sucking in a deep breath. Her red curls smelled delicious. They smelled like home. "I want to get better. I do."

And I did. We just disagreed on what I needed to get better.

She thought I needed a shrink. I thought I needed her. Why couldn't we agree to disagree? As long as I got better, that was all that mattered. And I would. I was.

Smoothing her hair back, I pressed my lips to her temple. Closing my eyes, I breathed her familiar scent in one more time. She still smelled like sunshine and happiness. Everything I'd ever wanted, and more.

Memories of us laughing in the car, making love on the beach, riding my Harley, and surfing hit me harder than a bitch slap. I missed that. Missed the "us" we used to be so damn badly. The emptiness inside my soul was killing me. Even worse than when I'd been blown up by an IED on a mission overseas.

Slowly, she lifted her face to mine and slid her hands up to my shoulders. "I think you can get better, and you will. I'll be here for you, as your wife, for whatever you need. And as long as you've stopped with the pills and the drinking—if you were drinking?" I shook my head, and she continued. "As long as you can quit those things, and accept that you need to get help again, then you'll get better. And I'll always be here for you. You know that."

I rested my head on hers again. It was easier than looking at her right now. I felt like such a failure. So weak. "I miss you so much, Ginger. So fucking much."

"I miss you, too," she said, letting go of me and stepping back.

In that moment, I hated myself. For hurting her. For lying to her. For being me. She'd be better off if she hated me. It would be so much easier if she did.

Even though I was trying to do the right thing by her, I wanted to go in that bedroom with her and make her want me again. If I made love to her, maybe she'd forget all about my troubles. Maybe she'd love me again and stop talking about how I needed help, if I had a chance at touching her. Maybe she'd forget about how much of a fuck-up I was and love me anyway.

That was the most selfish thing I'd ever thought...

But it didn't stop me from thinking it.

She walked toward the bedroom. "I'll take the couch tomorrow night."

"No, you won't." I fisted my hands at my sides, fighting the urge to follow her into that room with everything I had. "I'll take the couch every night, and you'll sleep in the bed. End of story."

"Finn—"

I clenched my teeth, rubbing my aching thigh. "Go to bed before I change my mind about letting you go to bed alone. I'm trying to do the right thing for once in my fucking life. Let me."

She didn't say anything. Just shut the door behind her.

And I was alone. Again.

chapter

six

Carrie

Early the next morning, I fluffed my hair and stared at myself in the mirror, critically measuring up my appearance. I had huge bags under my eyes from crying myself to sleep last night, and every other night before that. Ever since Finn had left, that had been my routine. Crying until I finally passed out from exhaustion.

Sleeping with his pillow. His shirt.

Anything that smelled like him, or used to smell like him.

Every time he touched me, it got harder to remember why he'd left. It got harder to remember the pain he'd caused by his lies, and instead I remembered the pain I felt because he was gone. But he'd admitted he needed help last night. That had to count for something, and I knew it. It was a step in the right direction.

One we'd needed very badly.

I smoothed the soft cashmere teal sweater I'd chosen to wear over my stomach, took a deep breath, tucked my hair behind my ear, and picked up my phone.

After taking a calming breath, I dialed my dad. It rang three times.

"Hello?" Dad asked. "Carrie?"

"Yeah. It's me." I gripped the phone. "How's Susan?"

"She's great. Right now, she's playing with Mom. She bought her a little pretend tea set, but Susan is more interested in stacking them up than she is in making tea."

I smiled. "Yeah, she's a little too young for that kind of play."

"I know." He laughed. "But you know how your mother is."

"I do." I hesitated. "But Susan's okay?"

"Of course." He fell silent. "Are you okay?"

"Yes." I paced across the bedroom. "This place is beautiful, Dad."

"Finn treating you like a princess?"

I looked at the empty bed. Half of it was perfectly smooth, and the other half was a mess. I'd been tempted to sneak out last night to steal his shirt or something, but I hadn't dared. I'd missed his scent last night. Missed *him*. Having him right on the opposite side of the door had only made that aching hollowness inside of me even louder.

Swallowing hard, I tried not to get all emotional on my father. That wouldn't help matters. "He always does."

"That's why we all love him so much," Dad said. "Now go have a romantic morning with your husband. Don't worry about us. I love you, Princess."

I chewed on my lower lip. "I love you, too, Dad."

Straightening my spine, I walked to the bedroom door and opened it. Three steps into the living room, I froze. Finn had his shirt off, and he was tending the fire. His hard muscles flexed and rolled as he poked the wood, and his ink swirled over the sinews. The veins in his arms stuck out, and he didn't see me, so I looked my fill while I could.

Before he saw me looking, and realized just how easily he could get me to forget everything he'd done with a simple kiss, I glanced away. But I'd never get sick of looking at him. Of studying every single hard edge of his body.

His light brown hair was messy, as if he'd just woken up, and his dark blue jeans were loose around his hips. He hadn't buttoned them up, so the "just woke up" appearance must have been legit. I swallowed hard, watching him with a hunger I couldn't deny.

After he finished tending the fire, he set the poker next to the fireplace and leaned against the mantle on one hand. His shoulder muscles bunched and hardened as he rubbed his injured leg. He winced and stopped, pressing his hand against his thigh.

And just like that, lust became concern.

My heart clenched tight. Instead of admiring his lean body, I saw the bags under his eyes. Saw the exhaustion and loneliness echoing in those blue eyes of his. I saw how far he'd fallen, and I knew I needed to pull him back into the light. It was on me this time. I couldn't fail him again.

Not like last time.

This time, he wouldn't have to leave me to get better. I could be his rock. I could be his person. I would help him, support him, and love him while he sought treatment. And he'd get better. He *had* to get better.

He hissed and rubbed his leg, paling as he did so. He was in pain, and he couldn't take anything for it. I couldn't imagine how that must feel. He was stuck in this endless cycle of pain from his injury and unable to do anything for it.

"Does it still hurt?" I asked.

He jumped, and turned to face me. As he swiped his forearm across his sweaty forehead, he nodded once. "Like hell."

"Want a Tylenol? I have some in my purse."

He flexed his jaw. "No."

"But I can—"

"I don't want any pills. You've got enough to hold against me. I don't need anything else," he gritted. "So, *no*, Carrie. I don't want a fucking pill."

I bit my tongue. I hated that he thought I was so unreasonable that he couldn't take a Tylenol, but I didn't dare push it. He pushed off the fireplace mantle and sank onto the couch, still bare-chested. My eyes fell on the tattoo he'd gotten for us, way back when we'd been dating. It said: "The sun is finally shining." Our code words for "I love you," back when we couldn't say it in front of my father. Our whole relationship had started with lies and secrets. It shouldn't be a surprise that we were here again, but it was. It really was.

I stared at him, not sure what to say. My husband was pure muscle, hotness, and sex. Everything about him screamed pleasure—from his hard shoulders, to his chiseled abs, to his narrow waist that tapered down to that V that made smart girls dumb.

That little V had worked on me all those years ago. It still did. And that wasn't even including those bright blue eyes of his, and all that hot ink…

"Ginger?" he said, his voice seductive and sweet.

I quickly looked back into his eyes. "Yeah?"

"If you don't stop stripping the rest of my clothes off with your eyes, I won't be responsible for my actions. I'm going to have to fuck you so hard, you'll sit uncomfortably for the rest of the day." He leaned forward, resting his elbows on his knees. "Remember that time in Mexico, when we made love on the balcony, overlooking the ocean and the stars? This could blow that time away. Think about that."

I swallowed a moan, remembering that night all too clearly. He'd taken me from behind and made me come numerous times. I'd limped for two days afterward. It had been wonderful. But then I forced myself to remember something else: The way he'd pulled back from me yesterday. He hadn't felt ready then, so he probably wasn't ready now.

Averting my eyes for a second, I muttered, "I'll stop."

"Pity." He glanced down at my mouth before moving back up to my eyes. "It would've been fun reminding you why we should be naked and in that bed where you slept all alone last night. Think I could make you come before I had you naked?"

Heck yeah, I did. "Finn…"

He stood up and came over to me, his hand skimming down my lower back and over the side of my butt. "I bet I could take these off and have you screaming out in pleasure within thirty seconds. Want to test me out? Take me for a test drive? See if I've lost my touch?"

"We shouldn't. Yesterday…" I broke off. "You weren't ready."

"Yeah, well, today is another day." He backed off, sitting down again. He sighed and glanced up at me sheepishly. "And I'm sorry I snapped at you earlier."

I stepped closer. "It's okay."

He rested his head back against the couch, swallowing hard and stretching his leg out in front of him. "And I'm all right. I just need a second."

I watched him, torn in indecision. Lies or no lies, this was the man I loved. I'd loved him for more than nine years, ever since I'd been that nineteen-year-old girl all alone on the beach at night, and I'd love him forever, no matter what happened. I wanted to *help* him. Slowly, I crossed the room and sat beside him.

He glanced at me from under his lashes and stiffened when I closed my hands around his upper thigh. "I'm going to rub it. Let me know if it hurts," I said.

"You don't have to do that," he said from between clenched teeth.

"I want to do it. I want to help you," I said, staring him right in the eye. "Please. Let me do this for you."

He nodded once, his jawline hard and unyielding.

I started rubbing, unable to ignore the hard muscles beneath my fingers, no matter how hard I tried. He'd always been so faithful to me. So loyal. He had so many good qualities, and it was hard to ignore them.

Even in the face of his issues, it was impossible to pretend those outstanding qualities didn't exist. There was no white and black with us. It was all gray.

So much freaking gray.

When I rubbed his thigh harder, he groaned and closed his eyes. I almost didn't hear him say: "You have questions about why I did what I did."

It wasn't a question, but I answered anyway. "Well...yeah. Of course I do."

"So ask me," he said, still not opening his eyes.

"I don't want to." I lowered my head and rubbed harder. "You've accused me of bringing my job home, and I don't want to push. I don't want you to think I'm doing that. Ever."

"I shouldn't have said that, because it's not true. You never do that, so I'm sorry for saying that, too." He caught my chin, tipping my face up so I met his eyes. His were somber and clear. "Ask me anything you want. I want to answer."

"But it'll lead to a fight," I whispered.

I was so sick of the fighting. Of the pain. Of it all.

"Then we'll fight." He kissed me gently. "And then we'll make up. We always do. But if we're going to move on, we need to get it all out so it doesn't fester and boil over into a huge fucking mess. That's the healthy thing to do."

I gave him a small smile and brushed his hair off of his face. It was so soft. I'd said that to so many patients so many times that I recognized it for what it was. A lesson he'd gotten from his therapist. I wanted to kiss that woman right now. "You're so smart."

"I know." He gave me a lopsided smile. "Now let's talk it out."

After taking a deep breath, I asked, "How long were you taking the pills? Were there more than the three bottles?"

"No, it was only the three. I was using them for less than a week. I know I shouldn't have done it, shouldn't have taken the chance." He turned to me again, his blue gaze piercing into mine. "But I just wanted to shut the voices up for a little while. I keep seeing them, all those men, dying over and over again. All day and night. It never stops." He looked away. "I thought if I could manage the pain, I could get a grip on everything else. I thought I'd be able to control the memories and the pain and the nightmares."

I nodded, my heart breaking for him. "I didn't know you had slipped back into that place."

"You didn't ask me," he said, his voice matter of fact. "Did it ever occur to you that I might have a relapse? Or did you just assume I was all better, and I'd never slip up again?"

"Of course I did. I always worry about you. About everyone I love." I glanced away. "But I was trying to give you privacy. Trying to trust you."

"I know." He covered his face. "But I'm curious, and I have to ask this. Did you notice I'd been acting differently at all?"

I crossed my arms defensively. He'd been acting strangely, yes, but I'd been too caught up in my own issues to notice. Trying to pay the bills. My ever-growing sickness. The stress of worrying about a husband who'd been injured way too many times. "Not really, no. But if you hadn't hid things from me, lied to me, I would have known."

"I know that. You think I don't fucking know that? But I'm your husband, and you told me to get out." He snapped his fingers. "Just like that."

I forced myself to keep my voice calm, even though I was upset, too. This was about him, not *me*. "What was I supposed to do after I got that call from the pharmacy? After you lied to me, straight to my face?"

"You were supposed to ask me why I'd done it. Talk to me. *Help* me." He shook me off and stood up, a hand behind his neck and the other balled at his side. "We're fucking married. We have a kid together, and you just shook me off like an unwanted bill or some shit like that. Who does that to the person they swore to love forever?"

My heart twisted painfully. Hearing him say it like that, it sounded awful. But after all he'd put me through in the past with his drug issues, I'd felt as if I hadn't had a choice. "I tried to talk to you that night. Tried to get you to talk to me. To admit the truth. Or did you forget that?"

"Of course not," he said, blanching. "But I was still h—"

He broke off. He obviously didn't want to say it out loud.

"Say it." I grabbed his hands. "You have to say it."

"No." He shook his head frantically and stood up. "*No*."

"Fine. I'll say it for you. You were still *high*." I lifted my chin. "What did you expect from me when confronted with that?"

"*Love*. I expected love! It's your fucking job to help people get through this shit. To be understanding and kind in the face of their plight. You're a fucking therapist. You get paid to help people like me heal." He yanked on his hair. "But your own husband has a small slip into hell over the space of eight fucking years, and you're done? You have no idea how much that hurt me, knowing you could get rid of me like that without blinking. How *mad* that made me."

I swallowed hard. All this time I'd been so angry with him, and I'd had no idea he had all this anger against me. I'd just assumed he was hurt, not mad.

How naïve of me.

"I'm sorry for that," I whispered, pressing a hand to my aching heart. "I didn't mean to make you think it was easy for me, because it wasn't. Not at all. It was the hardest thing I've ever done, because I *need* you in my life."

He completely ignored the last part, and said, "It didn't look like it was that hard for you from my angle," he said, his voice hard. "It looked like you'd been waiting for an excuse to kick me out, and you finally got it. And here I thought we'd been happy."

I threw my hands up. "We were. Which is why I can't figure out why you felt the need to take those pills behind my back. Or why you didn't tell me you were having flashbacks again. Why weren't you honest with me about it?"

He made a frustrated sound. "Because I was scared you'd flip out on me. That you'd think I was going to fall back into my old habits of drinking booze and popping pills. I was scared to revive bad memories of my dad dying, and the injuries, and the PTSD, and everything else that happened at that time in my fucking life. But most of all, I was ashamed to admit that I'd fallen down again."

I swallowed hard. That time in our life had been horrid. We'd had so many arguments, and he'd been suffering from PTSD on top of everything else. It was the darkest part of his life, and he was right. Finding him with those pills in his hand had brought me right back to that time. Right back to the past.

"Finn..."

He dropped his arms at his sides. "I was so fucking scared of losing you. I thought I'd be able to keep track of when I needed the pills. Thought I'd be okay if I could get a grip on that part of my life, if nothing else. Thought it would help me heal."

"I could've helped you do it." I tipped my head back. "If you'd come to me, none of this would have happened."

"I wasn't exactly thinking clearly, Ginger." His jaw ticked. "You should know what that's like. Why didn't you take more time to talk to me that night? Why did you kick me out? I never thought you'd do that to me. To us." He sat down again, looking defeated and alone. "Why didn't you stand by me?"

I wrapped my arms around my stomach. There were reasons I'd acted the way I'd acted that night, but he didn't need to know them yet. We were in enough of a mess already. One more stressor might put him over the edge. "I thought it was what you needed to hear. All actions have reactions, and—"

"Don't pull those cliché therapist sayings on me. I've heard them all already."

I nodded once, knowing he was right. I hadn't even realized I'd been saying it, because I'd been too busy panicking inside. He couldn't know my news yet. It might push him further into the black hole he was trying to fight his way out of. He'd been happy about Susan, but I couldn't assume he'd be happy about this one.

Not when he was barely able to hold on to what he already had, and I could see the worry in his eyes even now. He might not be ready to admit it, but he was worried about himself. About us. Most of all, about Susan. His denying the need for help scared me more than he ever did.

Not admitting you needed help when you did was terrifying.

I trusted Finn with all my heart. I did. But when he was in the grips of PTSD, Finn wasn't *Finn*. He was almost a stranger with a gun…and that scared me.

"And you know what else? There's nothing you could do that would send me running like that," he said, continuing. He had no idea how many thoughts were flying through my head right now. He sat beside me, our bodies touching, and locked gazes with me again, his blue eyes earnest. "I could walk in on you holding a bloody knife over a dead body, and I'd ask you where you wanted to hide the fucking body."

"I know. That's how you are."

"So why did you send me away?" he asked again.

"*I don't know!*" I'd been scared to lose him again, scared he'd break me again, but more importantly, I'd been scared he might do the same to our children. And I couldn't allow that to happen. "All I know is I couldn't go through all that pain again. We're not kids anymore, Finn. We have a family to worry about, and I can't put our family through all that pain all over again. While losing you is one of the worst things I can possibly imagine, I have to do what's best for everyone. Not just you."

He shook his head and cupped my cheek, stroking my skin gently. His tenderness hit me hard, and I realized how much I'd needed it. Needed this. He kissed me once. Twice. Three times. "But I can't lose you, Ginger. I've lived life without you, and I've lived it with you. I know which one is better. And I always have. I need you."

"I need you, too." I clasped his forearms. "So much. But I'm scared of what could happen."

"I am too," he whispered, his fingers flexing on me. "But if you just keep pulling me closer, and reminding me what I could lose, I'll get better. I swear it. And I know it's true, because I can't lose you again. I just can't."

Instead of immediately shutting him out, as I knew I should, I looked deep into his eyes. I could see his sincerity, and I knew that he knew he needed help. I knew he would eventually admit it, but I didn't know when. I did know one thing for sure, though. In a sea of uncertainty and fears, I loved him with all my heart. And he loved me, too.

Instead of telling him why I couldn't let him in, I just wanted to love him. Show him I hadn't given up on him. On us. I blinked back tears. "Then don't. Don't lose me."

Closing my eyes, I took a deep breath, and then I did it.

I pulled him in closer.

chapter
seven

Finn

I hadn't meant it in a literal sense—my words about her pulling me in closer. But when she did, I didn't question it or hesitate. No, sir. Instead, I closed my mouth over hers, taking control from her. This is how it always was with us. One second, we would be fighting, and the next we would be all over each other.

Maybe we'd actually be okay. Maybe love would be enough.

She had the power to heal me. She just had to believe.

My tongue slid over hers, and she whimpered into my mouth, her grip on me tightening. I pressed closer, growling and deepening the kiss as I did so. Her hand drifted over my bare back, sending shafts of need and pleasure coursing through my veins. It had been so long, too long, and I needed to have her. To claim her as mine.

To *own* her.

I ended the kiss, our heavy breathing the only sounds in the room. I ended the kiss, nibbling on her lower lip. "Fuck, you taste good."

"Are you okay?" She cupped my face. "Or should we stop?"

Taking a second, I thought about it. Actually thought about it. When she kissed me, the voices went away. So did the fear. I felt human again. So fucking human. She was my own personal medication. "I'm good. You're still on the pill, right? The last thing we need right now is

45

a baby getting in the mix."

She hesitated but nodded. "Yeah, we're good."

"Ginger..." I'd noticed the hesitation. The second of doubt that had crossed her mind. "You have to tell me you want this. Tell me you want me. There can be no doubt."

"Yes." She nodded frantically, trailing her fingers down my chest and over my abs. "I want this. I want you. I miss you so much, Finn."

Fucking A.

I swept her into my arms and carried her to the bed. I'd been fantasizing about her sleeping in the damn thing all night long, and now I was going to thoroughly fuck her in it. I laid her down gently, my gaze skimming up her slim body. She'd had a baby only a year ago, and she looked fucking perfect. I loved the stretch marks on her stomach, the ones she'd gotten from carrying our child. There were just two little ones, right above her belly button, but I fucking loved them.

They were her own personal battle scars.

Her body had changed, too, but for the better. Her hips were rounder. Her breasts fuller. Everything about her was perfection, and I'd never get enough. I don't think she'd ever realize exactly what she did to my body, mind, and soul — not to mention my heart.

She'd saved me.

And now she had the power to destroy me.

Lowering my body on top of hers, I kissed her hard, not wasting time with soft kisses and caresses. I needed her too damn badly, and she needed me. She arched her back beneath me, her muscles tight and hard. Slipping my hand under her ass, I lifted her closer to my hard cock, needing to feel her against me.

"Fuck, I missed you." I kissed the side of her neck, inhaling the floral scent of her long red hair, leaving a trail of kisses all the way down to her shoulder. Then I bit her, making her cry out in pleasure. Her nails dug into my back. "So." Another nibble on her shoulder. "Damn." Lower, on the top of her breast. "Much."

"*Finn.*" She gripped my shoulders, arching her back. "Now."

"Uh-uh." I kissed her neck again, tugging her sweater down a little bit. "That's not how you ask me for something."

"Please." She dug her nails in deeper. "*Please* take me."

I lowered myself over her body, lifting her sweater up inch by inch as I did so. "I don't know. It's been too long..."

"Which is why I need you *now*." She yanked on my hair. "Right now, *please*."

I *tsked*. "Not yet."

I undid her pants button and unzipped them. She squirmed beneath me, her eyes shut tight. "Finn..."

Yanking them down to her knees, I slipped my fingers between her thighs and brushed up against her wet pussy. "You're so ready. So hungry." I slid my fingers inside her black satin panties, running my finger over her clit gently. "So *mine*."

She opened her thighs. "I always will be. Just take me."

I withdrew my hand, grinning when she let loose a string of curses that would make a sailor blush. Slowly, I removed her pants the rest of the way and tossed them over my shoulder. Picking up her ankle, I nipped the tender skin there. She squirmed, a silly little grin on her face that did odd things to my heart.

"Even your ankle tastes good. Every inch of your body does." I nipped her thigh a little harder than necessary, and she let out a strangled groan, wiggling her sweet little ass at the same time. "I would know, since I've tasted you everywhere."

I moved higher up her thigh, and she froze, her entire body tense with anticipation. Mine responded automatically to hers, also revving up for the pleasure it knew was coming. And with my Carrie, the pleasure would be out of this world.

I knew that.

When I sucked on the sensitive inner thigh right below her panty line, she gasped and gripped me so tight it hurt. It felt fucking amazing. "Oh my God, Finn."

"Ask me." I flicked my tongue over her slit, tasting her through the thin fabric. She loved it when I made her beg, and I fucking loved it when she begged me. "Ask me *nicely*."

"P-Please taste me." She lifted her hips higher, demanding more. Demanding me. She bit down on her lower lip. "Please make me come."

Since she asked nicely...

I ripped her panties off with one swift pull and spread her thighs wide. Settling between her legs, I stared down at her soft pink pussy. She was so wet and perfect, and I'd missed her so damn much. Missed everything about her. I didn't think she'd ever truly understand how much I needed her in my life to be...well, *me*.

Lowering my mouth to her clit, I sucked her in deep and trailed my fingers over her slit, teasing her entry. Her intoxicating flavor washed over me, and I closed my eyes. I lost myself in pleasuring her. Man, I loved the way she squirmed right before she came, all frantic and crazy until she finally froze—my name on her lips and in her thoughts.

I'd get her there soon.

"*Finn*." She buried her hands in my hair, holding on securely. "Oh my God, yes. Please. *Yes*."

I thrust a finger inside her, crooking it just right, and she screamed, arching her back and breathing heavily. She was so fucking close. Too close. I wasn't ready to let her come yet. The waiting made it all the more sweet.

Pulling back, I flicked my tongue over her one last time. She tensed, digging her fingers into my scalp and holding me in place. "No, don't stop. Please. *Please* let me come."

"No." I nipped at her hip. "Not until I say you're ready."

She growled with frustration, but her eyes danced with excitement. She loved it when I told her no, but only in the bedroom. The rest of the time, she hated it.

She yanked on my hair. "*Finn.*"

"Hmm?"

"*Now.*" She curled her leg around my upper body, holding me close. "I'm dying. I need this. I need you."

My heart clenched at her words. I knew she meant she needed me to make her come, but there had been a time when she'd needed me in every way. I didn't think she did anymore, even if she didn't realize it yet. She'd sent me away once, and I had to keep my head on straight so it didn't happen again.

"Not yet." I closed my mouth around her nipple, biting down gently. She tightened her grip on my head, a small groan escaping her. "Not until I say you're ready."

"Oh my God," she said, tossing her head to the side. "*Please.*"

I scraped my teeth over her again, and she jerked. I pulled back, my eyes narrow. I hadn't been *that* fucking rough. "You okay?"

"Y-Yes." She squirmed. "I'm fine."

"Okay..."

"More." She yanked on my hair impatiently. "Now."

I closed my palms over her breasts, rolling my thumbs over her hard nipples. They still fit in my hand perfectly. "Ask me nicely," I said, my tone deceptively soft.

"Please. *Please* make me come."

I kissed a path down her stomach and nibbled on the spot right above the tiny patch of red curls she'd left for me. Her stomach twitched. "But it's been so long."

"Which is why I need you." She pushed my head down a little bit, and I let her. "It's been *too* long."

I licked her slowly, taking my time. She dug her nails into my scalp. It hurt like fuck—and I loved every second of it. So I did it again, and slapped her ass playfully. She liked when I did that. "God." She whimpered. "*Please*, Finn."

"Now," I demanded, closing my mouth over her clit.

Slowly, I rolled my tongue over her in the way that was guaranteed to drive her insane. Guaranteed to send her over the edge. Her thighs opened wide, and then she clenched them tightly on my head. Her whole body arched and twisted and rolled, and I cupped her ass, squeezing hard. She stiffened, and her mouth fell open wordlessly.

"Finn," she finally breathed, collapsing against the bed. I let her. "Oh my God."

I nibbled on her hip one last time, then crawled up her body one slow inch at a time, dropping kisses as I went. When I reached her mouth, I kissed her, my tongue touching hers and sweeping inside her sweet mouth. She closed her arms around me, hugging me close. It felt so right. So perfect.

How could she have ever doubted that we were meant to be?

Anything that felt this good was meant to be.

It had to be.

I cupped her ass in my hands, lifted her hips slightly, and thrust inside of her. She cried out into my mouth, the sound pleading and desperate. I pumped my hips, slapping her ass one more time as I fucked her hard and fast. She needed it, and so did I. We both needed to get the release the other could give us, and then we could concentrate on taking it slow next time.

If there *was* a next time.

"Jesus, Carrie." I thrust inside her harder. "Fuck."

She cupped my face tenderly. "Kiss me."

I kissed her, moving my hips faster. She wrapped her legs around me, holding me close, and I closed my eyes, losing myself in her touch. Her kiss. Her smell. Everything.

She was my savior. She was my downfall.

Only she could save me from my demons.

My balls pulled tight to my body, and the pressure inside of me just kind of snapped. I drove inside of her one last time, and then I came explosively. She cried out, her pussy tightening on me as she came. I kept kissing her, refusing to stop.

Afraid that if I stopped the world might come to an end.

She broke off the kiss, gasping for air. I dropped my forehead on hers, keeping my eyes shut. I wasn't ready for her to see me yet. Wasn't ready to…

"I love you," she said, her voice heavy with emotion. "I love you so much."

I nodded, swallowing hard. "I love you, too."

I needed to pull my shit together before she realized how fucking broken I was right now. Before she saw right through me…

And left me again.

chapter
eight

Carrie

I kissed his shoulder, my heart racing the whole time. Things had been so rough lately, but while we'd been in each other's arms like that...everything had felt *right*. As if we'd be okay, like we always were. But once the euphoria wore off, and I came crashing down to Earth again, the obstacles in front of us came back into view.

He was already so emotionally off-balance, and I'd made love to him. That was a huge no-no, but I'd done it anyway. Would it make him backslide? Would he slip further into the abyss? I knew what I would tell a client, but I wasn't his therapist.

I was his wife, and that made everything different. There were emotions and fears and pain and love. The fear was the worst, though.

Last time he'd been this way, he'd left me because he'd been so far gone. Would he leave me again? He'd said he wouldn't, but that didn't stop the fear. It didn't stop me from worrying about him. I felt like we were tiptoeing that line we'd walked all those years ago, and I was terrified it would end the same way.

With us no longer together.

Please, God, let us stay together.

He shuddered and pushed off me. Dragging a hand through his hair, he stood. He looked nervous, which made me nervous. "Are you okay? No regrets?" he asked.

"No." I hugged my knees to my chest. "You?"

He shook his head. "I'm good."

We stared at each other wordlessly, the air between us tight with tension.

"I'm—"

At the same time, he asked, "Are you—?"

We both broke off.

I laughed uneasily. "You go ahead."

"Are you sure? You can go."

Hugging my knees tighter, I shook my head. "Nope, you go first."

"I was just going to ask if you're hungry." He tugged on the hair at the back of his head. The same hair I'd been pulling on earlier as he drove me crazy. "I can cook some omelets, if we have the ingredients."

My stomach growled loudly. I pressed a hand to it and smiled shyly. "Um, judging from the T-rex sounds coming from my stomach, I guess I'm hungry, so yeah."

He laughed. "All right." He stepped into his jeans, leaving his boxers crumpled up on the floor. "I'll hook you up before the monster tears through your belly."

"Thank you," I said, my voice soft.

He glanced at me, almost in surprise. "You're welcome. What were you going to say earlier?"

"I wanted to make sure you're okay." I took a deep breath. "That what we did and said weren't making it worse."

His blue eyes blazed with so much emotion it could cut the air. "There will never be a day where making love to you makes me feel worse, Ginger. Never."

With that, he walked out the door and into the living room. I watched him go, sitting naked on the bed we'd just made love in. I stood up shakily, pressing a hand to my stomach. We had to find a way to make this work, for everyone. For our little family.

I turned to the side, studying my stomach.

Already I could see the slightest of protrusions. It was probably just my imagination, and no bigger than when I'd had a big meal, but still. I *saw* it. I'd found out I was pregnant the same night I'd found out he was suffering again. I hadn't had the chance to tell him yet.

How long would it be before he saw it, too?

Part of me was worried it might make his fight even harder—knowing he had yet another person relying on his ability to heal. But it could go the other way, too. It could give him another reason to get better. To get help. But could I take that chance? Could I tell him, and just hope for the best, when he was already struggling?

I couldn't, but I'd have to do it at some point.

Eventually, he'd notice.

Straightening my spine, I dressed again. When I came out of the bedroom, he was busily whipping the eggs in a bowl. A pepper, tomato, and onion sat on the cutting board, waiting for a dicing. Coffee brewed in the pot, and I looked at it enviously.

I'd given it up the second I'd gotten that positive pregnancy test.

"Hey." He shot me a small smile and headed for the pot. "You look like you need this."

I smiled and smoothed my hair, taking the coffee from him even though I wouldn't drink it. I'd pretend to drink it, and then dump it once his back turned. I felt guilty about the secret I was holding close to my chest, but I had to make sure it would help him, not hurt him. I had to be sure before I opened my mouth.

But still, it felt wrong.

"Thanks." I blew on the steamy beverage. "Need some help?"

"Nah, you sit and take it easy." He glanced at me from under his thick brown eyelashes. "I got this."

I smiled and sat at the bench by the island. "Okay."

He slid the metal bowl to the side and picked up a big knife. "We had all the fixings, after all."

"Good." I set my coffee down untouched. "I called Dad and checked on Susan. She's doing good."

He chopped a tomato in half. "I'm sure she's getting spoiled as hell right now."

"Of course." I tapped my finger on the rim of my mug. "Could we expect anything else?"

He laughed. "Never."

Something bumped outside the door, and Finn broke off. He didn't even hesitate or take a second to think. Instantly, he reached for the spot where his gun had been. The panic that hit his eyes when he realized he was unarmed was gut-wrenching.

"It was just the wind," I hurried to say, trying to soothe away his fears before they fully came to the surface. "Finn, it's just —"

"You don't know that. It could be anyone. Anything." He snatched the knife up and stalked toward the door. "Whatever you do, don't follow me. Stay in the kitchen, behind the island. I need to keep you safe. You have to be safe."

My heart splatted on the hardwood floor right between my feet. He was back in that place again, where there was a threat around every corner. Where death lurked and so did devastation. I followed him, my eyes latched on his back, but kept my distance.

"It's happening again," he mumbled, his voice so low I barely heard it. "Not again. Never again."

I bit down hard on my tongue. He was breaking my heart. "There's no one there," I said softly. "It's just an episode putting you back in that place until you're not sure what's real and what isn't." I rested my hands on his back. He tensed underneath my touch. "We're not there. We're safe and sound."

His shoulders bunched. "What makes you so sure we aren't there? I swear I can *hear* them, Carrie." He rested his hands on the door. "They're right outside the door, and they need my help. I need to help them this time."

"There's no one there. It's just us."

"*Carrie*." He spun on me, his eyes wild and haunted, like a caged animal that had just been set free. He grabbed his head, the knife still in his hand, and stared at me with panicked blue eyes. "Make it stop. Help me."

I eyed the knife, but I trusted Finn enough to know he wouldn't hurt me, or our baby. And he needed me. I held my breath and wrapped my arms around him. He tensed even more, but I held on tight, resting my cheek on his chest. "Sh. It's okay. We're okay. We're safe."

His arms stayed at his sides, as if he didn't know how to hug me back, but then he did. He crushed me against his chest, the knife clattering to the floor. "I'm sorry." He buried his face in my neck and shuddered. "I'm sorry. I'm sorry. I'm sorry."

I choked back a sob. Seeing him like this, so lost, hurt so much. "It's okay. There's nothing to be sorry for. Nothing at all."

"I'm such a fucking mess right now." He let out a long breath. "Shit, Carrie, I can't do this to you. Not again."

"You're not doing anything to me." I kissed his heart. The heart I loved so much. "You're such a good man, Finn Coram. Don't you ever think otherwise. Don't you ever doubt it."

He made a broken sound. "You deserve better. You deserve more."

"That's not true at all. I can't think of anyone else I'd rather be with. Ever. I want you as my husband, my lover, and my best friend. You're all I need." I smiled up at him, trying to show him with my words and my eyes and my smile that I meant every word. He had to know it. "And you're going to be okay. We're both going to be okay."

"I need you, Ginger." He took a shaky breath. When he looked down at me, the panic was gone from his eyes, but shame had taken its place. That broke my heart even more. He had nothing to be ashamed of. Nothing at all. "That's what I need."

I forced a big smile. "You have me. Always have. Always will."

"I know. I'm sorry I did that. Sorry if I scared you."

He had, but I'd never admit it. "Please. I watch horror movies at night, by myself, when it's storming outside. I'm not scared of a small dose of reality."

"Good." He studied me closely. Too closely. "Because if it ever gets to be too much…"

"It won't." I squeezed his biceps. "Ever. I'm here for you."

He rubbed his eyes. "And I know that. I do. I'm just so fucking *exhausted* and I can't sleep. I keep hearing things that aren't there. Seeing things that don't exist anymore. It's slowly driving me insane."

Then he needed a nap, and I'd make sure he got one. "Why don't you go in the bathroom and splash some water on your face?" I said, keeping my tone soothing. "I'll lock the front door and wait for you in the kitchen."

"Right. Okay," he said, his voice an echo of the real him. "I'll be right back."

He headed for the bathroom, and I made a mental note to help him sleep later on. He needed it. Needed a clear head to fight off the demons that wouldn't leave him alone. I wish I could fight them off for him. Wish I were strong enough to scare them away, so he could have some peace and quiet. Wished I could help him.

As soon as the bathroom door shut, I picked up the knife off the wood floor and went into the kitchen. I passed my seat by the island and set the knife down on the island again. With a hollow stomach, I picked up my coffee mug, dumping the contents into the sink.

After I washed it down the drain with some water, I gripped the counter edge tightly. Everything was such a mess, and I liked to think I had it under control, but this was my husband we were talking about. I couldn't look at him objectively. He wasn't some patient I saw twice a week in my office. None of this was under my control.

Not him. Not me. Not his condition.

And it was freaking terrifying as hell.

When he came back out, I forced a bright smile and asked, "Feel better?"

"Yeah." He nodded and rubbed his eyes. He looked exhausted. "Thanks for talking me down. I don't know what I'd do without you."

I swallowed hard. Was I really helping him? Or was I making it worse, like I had before? Last time he'd had to leave me to get better. What made this time any different?

I smiled wider. "You're welcome."

"Seriously, Carrie." He came up to me and tipped my head back. He swallowed hard, his Adam's apple moving with emotion. "You have no idea how much you've saved me. How strong you are. I admire that about you. So damn much."

I blinked away the looming tears. God, I was so emotional with all these darn hormones raging through my body. "You're strong, too."

He smiled. "I love you."

"I love you, t—" My stomach growled loudly, and I pressed a palm to it. "Oops. Sorry."

He laughed. The sound was musical and healing and so very him. I'd missed that sound more than words could ever express. "Maybe I should get back to cooking before you start taking bites out of me," he said, his blue eyes dancing with amusement.

"You'd love it if I took a bite out of you," I retorted, keeping my voice light and free. He needed me to be strong for him. Needed a break from his demons. "And you know it."

"You're right. I would." He kissed me on the forehead as he passed by me. "But if my lady is hungry, then I have to feed her. It's my husbandly duty."

I followed him; rubbing the goose bumps his kiss had given me off my arms. "I am pretty hungry," I admitted. "We never ate dinner last night."

"Shit." He rubbed his jaw. "You're right. We kind of got caught up in the moment of leaving. You turned off the stove, right?"

"Yeah. I just dumped the pasta instead of eating it. I wasn't hungry."

He picked the knife back up and resumed chopping. Halfway through the onion, he froze. He glanced at the sink, my coffee mug, then me. "You drank all your coffee?"

I averted my eyes. "Yeah. When you were in the bathroom."

"Okay." He still watched me closely. Too closely. "Want more?"

"No. I'm good." I tucked my hair behind my ear and slid onto the stool. "If I drink more than my one cup, I'll get all jittery and hyper. No one wants that."

His lips tilted up at the corners. "I, for one, like when you're hyped up on caffeine. It's funny. And, sometimes, you get horny and take advantage of me in dirty, *dirty* ways."

I snorted. "Is that so?"

"Yep." He stared me down. "Feeling dirty now?"

I pointed at the half-cut onion. "Nope. I'm feeling hungry."

"Fine." He sighed dramatically and set back to work. "I'll slave away on this, then, if you promise to be dirty later."

I laughed. "We'll see about that *after* you take a nap. You need a nap."

He glanced up at me, the expression in his eyes so tender and loving that it stole my breath away. Literally, stole my breath away. I clenched my hands in my lap and gave him a small smile back. "If you want me to nap, then I'll try my best. For you."

I gave him a small smile. "I do."

"But then after..." He reached out and tugged on a piece of my hair. It sent desire spiraling to the pit of my stomach. "You're mine to do with as I please. Understood?"

In the flash of one second's time, he went from loving to sexy. And the way he was looking at me now...it made me sure of one thing. I understood, all right.

And I couldn't wait.

chapter nine

Finn

Later that night, I stood in the kitchen, watching Carrie from behind. I'd slept most of the afternoon away, and I felt more alive than I had in weeks. It had only served to prove my theory was right. One touch from her, and I'd slept like a fucking baby. She was the only thing I needed to get better. She was my anchor.

She would save me.

Earlier, I'd laid my head on her lap, and she'd massaged my temples until everything had faded away. She'd talked to me, her soft voice slowly sending me into the oblivion of sleep. And as I'd drifted off into dreamless slumber, I'd been sure I knew what heaven felt like.

It was Carrie holding me. Loving me.

When I'd woken up, she'd still been there, just like she'd promised. She gave me hope when hope had been lost. Maybe with her help, I'd pull through. Maybe we could go back to normal, and the voices in my head would shut the hell up. They'd stop crying out as they died, gurgling and choking on their own blood.

Maybe my head would be my own again.

I stepped closer to her, watching her intently the whole time. She had her usual romance book in her hand, and the fire played with the highlights of her red hair. Her lips were pursed together, and her eyes flew over the pages, her forehead wrinkled with concentration. It was the little things like this that got to me.

She was fucking pretty, sitting there, concentrating on her book. I never wanted to forget the way she looked, doing something as normal as enjoying a Saturday afternoon reading session. Or the way she always curled her ankle over mine in her sleep. Or how she hogged more than half the bed even though she was half the size of me. Or how she snorted when she laughed too hard.

Those were the things you missed the most when you lost someone. I'd learned that twice now in our lifetime.

She smiled, her eyes still on her book. Inexplicably, without me even knowing why she smiled, I smiled, too. That's how contagious her moods were. If she was happy, I was happy. If she was crying, then I was a fucking wreck. She didn't realize how much power she had over everything I did. Everything I thought.

My whole life revolved around her, and she didn't even know it.

"What's so funny?" I asked, coming around the front of the couch. I picked up her feet, sat down, and set her legs on my lap. We'd done this a million times before, but tonight it felt new. "Do share with the rest of the class."

She rested the book on her chest, her cheeks a fetching pink. I'd once teased her about how redheads weren't supposed to look pretty when they blushed, but she did. "I don't think a teacher would want me to read this book to the class."

I stared at the cover. It had a couple in the throes of passion on it. The man held the woman's wrists above her head with one hand, and her hair was fisted in the other. "This teacher does."

"I'm sure you do." She laughed. "But I'm not doing it."

"What's in these books anyway?" I reached for it, but she snatched it out of my reach, holding it above her head. "Hey, give me that."

"No way," she said, her eyes wide. "You can't read this."

"Why not?"

"Because it's...it's..." She looked at the book, then at me. "Dirty."

"Dirty?" I cocked a brow. "Like, really, *really* dirty?"

Her cheeks went even redder. "Yes."

"Then I must read it." I hauled her lower on the couch by her feet, and she shrieked. Hugging the book tight to her body, she kicked and squirmed, but I didn't release her. "I offer no quarter. Surrender, or suffer the dire consequences."

She rolled her eyes, the book still clutched tight to her chest. "What are the *dire consequences*?"

"You want to find out?"

"I'll take my chances." She white-knuckled the book. "I'm not scared of you."

I grinned. "That's your first mistake."

"Do your worst, sir," she said, her eyes flashing with challenge. And laughter. Man, I loved seeing that. It had been too long. It felt like fucking ages. "I will never surrender."

I laughed, loving this playful side of her that I hadn't seen since before we'd had Susan. Dropping my voice low and smothering on a Spanish accent, I said, "I am Finn Coram. You took my book from me. Prepare to die."

She pealed off into laughter at my *Princess Bride* reference—a favorite of hers— and I pounced. Knowing her weak spot, I went straight for the armpits, tickling her mercilessly. She lost herself in laughter even more, her squeals and cries mingling into curses and my name and pleas.

I laughed even harder, my fingers moving over her without mercy. "Surrender!"

"Oh—my—God." She arched her back, the laughter taking over again. "Uncle. I cry—*agh!*"

I tickled her even harder. "What's that again? I couldn't hear you."

"I said—*ahhhhhh.*"

I nibbled on her neck as I tickled her, breathing heavy and making weird noises. She laughed even harder. Finally, she dropped hold of the book, and it hit the floor. I rolled on top of her, pinning her body between the couch and me.

With one arm, I grabbed her wrists and held them over her head. Just like on the book cover. "Surrender, wench."

"Never," she said, tossing her head to the side and staring up at me with sparkling eyes.

Grinning, I smoothed her hair back from her eyes. "In case you didn't notice, I already won." With my free hand, I reached down and picked up the book. "Now…let's see here…"

"Oh my God," she moaned, closing her eyes. "You're killing me."

"Oooh, look. A dog-eared page." I *tsked* and opened it up. "Don't you know you're not supposed to do that to books?"

Her cheeks went even pinker. "Give it back to me."

I cleared my throat and read out loud. "Okay, here goes: *He pulled my hair and urged me to my feet. I hissed and grabbed his wrists, but truth be told, I loved it. I loved it when he played rough, and I loved it when he took control. It drove me insane knowing that I placed all my trust in him, and he didn't hurt me. Didn't fail me. Instead, he brought me endless amounts of pleasure. He dropped to his knees in front of me, biting the sensitive flesh above my core. When his tongue dipped lower, moving over my aching flesh, I —*"

She licked her lips, her eyes now locked on my mouth. "Finn."

A fist of desire hit me in the gut, and I tightened my grip on her wrists. I hadn't expected the words to be so...intoxicating. I didn't want to stop reading. I wanted to read the whole dirty scene to her since she'd obviously liked it enough to earmark it for easy reading.

I lowered the book and nipped the skin right below her ear. She shivered, her fingers clenching nothing above her head since I still held them in place. "Still want me to stop?"

She hesitated, but shook her head.

Thank fucking God.

I looked back down at the book, finding my spot quickly. "Where was I...ah, yes. *I cried out and my legs buckled under me. He slapped my ass, his voice harsh. 'I didn't say you could sit down.' He slapped me again, a little harder this time, and it hurt so good. 'Please, sir,' I begged, my panties getting so wet I could feel them. 'Take me. Love me.'"*

She made a small broken sound. "Keep going."

My cock thickened with need.

"'Not yet,' he said, his voice harder than his huge, bulging cock. 'You need to suffer for your disobedience first.' With that, he flipped me onto my stomach, pulled me ass first in the air, and caressed my bare flesh. Then ever so slightly, he traced the curve of my slit.'"

She wrapped her leg around my waist, opening herself up to me. I lowered the book, locking gazes with her. "Jesus, Ginger. You like this stuff?"

Licking her lips, she nodded. "I especially like it coming from your lips."

"Well, then." I scanned through the next couple of paragraphs, and what I saw made me even harder. Even more desperate for her. I tossed the book aside, and slipped my hand under her sweet ass. I tapped it gently. "Let's take it out of the fictional world, and make it real. You've been a bad girl. Ass in the air, Ginger."

She blinked at me. "Wh-What?"

"You heard me." I pushed off the couch and gripped my waistband. With a flick of my wrist, I undid the button. "I read what comes next in the book, and we're doing it. Ass. In. The. Air."

She blinked up at me and licked her lips. Her eyes were dilated with desire, and she had the most fetching pink blush across her cheeks. "O-Okay."

Standing up, she rested her hands on the top of the couch and spread her legs slightly. I skimmed my fingers over her ass cheek, my entire body throbbing with need. "So fucking hot."

She glanced over her shoulder coyly, wiggling her ass the slightest bit. "Thank you."

I lightly spanked her, no harder than I'd done earlier today in the bedroom. But it felt dirtier. She shuddered, her fingers flexing on the couch. "Thank you, *what*?"

"Finn."

"Nope." I smacked her again, the sound ringing through the silent room, intermingling with the sounds coming from the crackling fire behind us. "Try again."

A breathy moan escaped her. "*Sir?*"

"There you go." I caressed her ass, massaging the spot I'd smacked with a soothing hand, and my heart pounded against my ribs. "I like the sound of that on your lips. I'll expect you to say it again later when I'm making you come."

Her fingers tightened on the couch. "Yes, sir."

"Such obedience..." I closed my arms around her hips, grabbing the button on her jeans. "I like it. A man could get used to this."

"Don't expect it out of the bedroom," she said drily.

"Never." I fisted her hair, tugging ever so slightly until her head tipped back. "But in it...that's a different story. In it, you're mine."

She whimpered. "Yes."

"Now you need to get naked so I can spank that pretty little ass like you deserve," I demanded, pulling her hair a little harder. "You've been a bad girl, and it's time for your punishment."

She shivered and thrust her ass back, her long red hair cascading down her back and over my fist. "Oh my God, Finn. *Yes.*"

And with that, I released her hair, unsnapped her pants, and yanked them down to her knees. She didn't have anything on underneath. She was blissfully, perfectly, amazingly naked. "*Fuck.*"

I fell to my knees behind her.

chapter
ten

Carrie

I clasped the top of the couch tighter, closing my eyes. Finn was driving me crazy. Crazier than he ever had before, and that was saying a lot. He always drove me insane with want. Always made me crazy for him with nothing more than a look and a cocky smile. But this…

This was the stuff romance writers wrote about.

Only it was *real*.

After he pulled my pants down, he sank to his knees behind me, his hands on my bare hips. I bit down on my lip, dying to see what he did next. This escape, this release, was what we'd both needed. Yes, he had unresolved issues. And yes, we needed to work on them. But we also needed this. Needed to reconnect.

"Ginger…" He smoothed his hand over my butt, his touch tender and light. "You have no idea how hot you look right now. The things you do to me…"

I swallowed hard, my mind turning back on after the haze of desire he'd awoken with his naughty reading. He was my number-one priority right now, and this probably wasn't the best thing for him. "Are you sure you are okay to do this? Maybe we should just talk."

"No." He smacked me lightly; the sound a heck of a lot louder than

62

it should have been since he barely touched me. "I napped like you asked me to, and I told you all my feelings all fucking day long. Now it's time for my reward. It's time for me to have you."

I closed my eyes. "Finn, I—"

"Excuse me?" His hand stilled, a mere inch or so from where I needed him to be. "What did you just call me?"

My stomach twisted and turned into a million knots. The alpha dominance in his voice came straight out of the book, only hotter because it was Finn. "Sir."

"Better." He chuckled, the tone raspy and sexy. "Much better."

He slipped his hand between my thighs, rubbing up against my clit with his knuckles. It was a barely there touch, but the way he did it was freaking hot. "Oh my God."

"Uh-uh." He slid his hand between my thighs and separated my legs again. "I didn't say to do that. Don't fucking move unless I tell you to."

Before I could even form a reply, he bit the spot at the top of my thigh, right below my butt and toward my inner thigh. My knees buckled, and I almost fell, but somehow I managed to stay upright. He moved between my legs, parting me with his fingers. I was so exposed like this. So vulnerable.

But much like the character in the book that he'd read out loud to me, I knew that I could trust Finn to take care of me. To pleasure me in ways I'd never imagined before...and more. Despite everything, I knew I could trust him to take this submissiveness of mine, and not take advantage of it. Of me.

When he flicked his tongue over my clitoris, I cried out and dug my nails into the couch even more. Without warning, he slapped my ass lightly and went down on me, his tongue moving in slow, sensuous circles. His teeth scraped against me, adding a small measure of pain to the pleasure, and I tensed, my whole body already so freaking close to an orgasm that it wasn't even funny.

He must've sensed it, tasted it or something, because he pulled back and said, "No coming. Not yet. I'm gonna make you beg for it, just like your books."

And then he stopped. Just *stopped*. "What? No. I need—"

He stood, his hand on my butt. He gripped me tight, his fingers digging into the soft flesh there. "Excuse me? Are you talking back?"

"N-No." I licked my parched lips. "I just—"

He caressed my butt, his fingers gliding over the side and across my thigh. When he closed his hand over my core from behind, his fingers dipping inside me just enough to drive me crazy, I collapsed against his chest. "From now on, the only words allowed out of your mouth are *more, yes, please,* and *sir.* Got it?"

I nodded frantically, silently willing his fingers to move over me. To bring me to the edge again. "Yes, sir."

He withdrew, making me want to scream obscenities, but I bit down on my tongue to stay silent. Unless I wanted to beg him, I needed to stay silent. And just like he wanted me to beg him…I wanted him to earn my begging.

When I heard his belt come out of the loops of his pants, I sucked in a deep breath. I wanted to ask him what he was doing, but I didn't. I kept silent, because he'd told me to. A moment later, he tugged my pants off the rest of the way, and then he grabbed the hem of my shirt. "Arms up."

Without a word, I lifted my arms, and he pulled the shirt over my head.

He hissed in a breath through his teeth. "You were planning on teasing me later, weren't you? Wearing nothing under your clothes…"

"Yes, sir."

I could say more, like how I'd gotten the idea from him when he'd left his boxers on the floor, but that took more words than I'd been permitted to say. And I was *trying* to be a good girl so I could be rewarded.

He chuckled and ran his belt down my back. "Such a tease."

I silently bit my lip, waiting to see what he did next. God, *dying* to see what he did next. If he spanked me with it, I might convulse, shudder, and melt into a puddle on the wood floor never to be seen again. Seriously.

All of my professional training told me that this was a really bad idea, that even pretend violence could have ramifications, but it was Finn, and this was me, so I trusted him. My training had no place in my marital bed.

The belt dipped lower, over my butt, and he tapped me lightly with it. "You know what I do with teases?"

I ran through my permitted words, and opted for, "Sir?"

"I punish them." He smacked my rear with the leather belt, hard enough to sting a tiny bit, but not hard enough to actually hurt. He'd never actually hurt me. "And if they're good for that? They get rewarded very, *very* generously."

"Please, sir."

"So eager. So sweet." He fisted my hair, trailing the belt over my skin again. I whimpered. "You like that, Ginger?"

I tried to nod, but the movement pulled against his unyielding grasp.

He tightened his grip on me. "Answer me."

"Y-Yes, sir." I licked my dry lips again. "*Please*."

He slapped my butt with the leather, and he rubbed the spot tenderly afterward. The sting spread over me, making my thighs tremble and my whole body beg for more. I bit down on my tongue, a moan escaping despite my efforts to hold it back.

"You're so soft. So flawless." He dragged the belt over my stomach, creeping lower and lower until he abruptly stopped, right below my belly button. His hand covered the stretch marks I'd gotten from carrying our child. He said he loved them because they were my own battle wounds. Just like his. "I hate to touch you. To make you dirty. But then again…" He skimmed it across my belly. "I love it, too."

"P-Please, sir." I reached behind me, closing my fingers over his thighs. My fingertips rested on his butt. He was naked, too. Thank God. "*Please*."

He smacked my butt again, a little harder this time, and tossed the belt aside. From behind, he cupped my breasts, squeezing them and rolling his thumbs over their hard tips. I cried out, resting my back against his chest, and closed my eyes, losing myself in his touch. When his rough palms moved lower, over my stomach and down to cup my core again, he bit down on my neck.

His hard erection pressed against my lower back, and suddenly, I ached to taste him. To please him with my mouth. It had been so long since I'd done it that I couldn't even remember the last time. It was overdue. So much between us was overdue.

I spun in his arms, resting my hand on his chest. He let me. I locked gazes with him as I lowered myself to the couch. As I settled on the edge, he flexed his jaw and threaded his hands in my hair. Reaching out, I clasped his smooth shaft and closed my fist around it.

Then I looked up at him from beneath my lashes, moved closer so my mouth touched the tip, and asked, "Please, sir?"

"You asked so nicely." He ran his finger down my jaw, his touch soft yet possessive. He fisted his hand in my hair and urged me closer. "How could I say no to such a pretty request?"

Grinning, I opened my mouth and guided him in, closing my lips around him and sucking him in deep. He groaned and tossed his head back, his corded muscles tightening and teasing me. Every inch of his body was so hard. So perfect. And it was mine.

All *mine*.

I rolled my tongue over him, letting my eyes drift shut, and he moved his hips experimentally, going deeper into my mouth. I relaxed my throat and let him guide himself in, sucking and licking and loving every second of it. When he let out a strangled run of curses, his hand tugging on my hair impatiently, I sucked even harder.

Cupping his butt with one hand, I held him in place, and my other moved over his shaft as I sucked on the tip, licking up every drop he gave me. When his muscles went hard under my skin, and he cursed, I took him all the way in, covering his whole erection with my mouth.

"Jesus, Carrie." He fisted my hair and tugged. "Enough. I don't want to come like this. I want to be buried inside of your pussy when I come."

I sucked harder, refusing to give in.

He hissed, pulling my hair until my eyes stung with tears. Finally, I let go. He tugged me to my feet by the hair, and he bent down until our noses touched. "I said stop, and you didn't listen."

I licked my lips, already dying for another taste of him. "Sir?"

"You've been a bad, bad girl, Ginger." He caressed my cheek tenderly, the loving movement at odds with his words. "Time for your punishment."

He spun me abruptly, bending me over so my butt was in the air again. He gripped my hips, tilted them up, and thrust inside of me with one hard, quick push. I hadn't been expecting that, so I cried out in surprise—and pleasure.

So much freaking pleasure.

"*Yes.*" I gripped the couch so hard I swore I heard it tear. "Oh my God, yes."

"I didn't say you could say those words." He slid his hand up my body, resting it right below my throat possessively. "Should I stop? Punish you?"

"Please, sir." I gasped when he bit down on my shoulder, sending a shaft of pain to intermingle with the pleasure. "*Please.*"

"Please what?"

I whimpered, because there was no way to answer that with my permitted words. Oh, wait. I'd forgotten one. "More. More, more, *more.*"

"Abso-fucking-lutely," he murmured, biting down again and moving his hips with a precision that killed me. "You're allowed to come now."

"Please," I panted.

His free hand came down to massage my clit, sending me over the edge. As he made love to me from behind, his hands working their magic, I closed my eyes and lost myself in him. I exploded with pleasure, need, and so much want.

Everything just stopped, except this.

Him. *Us.*

He grunted and moved behind me, his hips pumping faster. Deeper.

Inexplicably, I crept toward the edge again, *thisclose* to coming a second time. His fingers moved over my clit as he made love to me, hitting a spot inside of me that sent shivers through my whole body. "*Yes!*"

My entire body tensed, and he went still behind me.

"Fuck," he muttered, pumping into me one more time. "*Carrie.*"

I was right there with him, coming a third time just from his fingers moving over me. He tightened his grip on me, keeping our bodies glued together, and fell on the couch, hauling me onto his lap effortlessly as he did so. I curled up like a sleepy kitten, and I might have purred.

He rubbed my hair back from my face, his breathing uneven and his hard chest and arms covered with a fine sheen of sweat. His hold, his touch, they were both so tender. So very Finn. I'd missed this. Missed him.

Dropping his forehead to my head, he sighed deeply. "See? I knew it. For a second there, after you made me leave, I thought I'd need help. But now that I'm back in your arms, I know I don't."

My heart shattered. Had he really just told me he had been planning on getting help, but he'd changed his mind because of me? No. Just *no*. "I'm not enough, Finn. I love you, and I'm here for you, but you need help. Help I can't give you."

"But I don't." He laughed freely, sounding so freaking happy. It only made it harder, because I knew he was wrong. And eventually, I'd have to tell him that. "You're all the medicine I need. As long as I have you here holding me, I'll be okay."

I swallowed hard, dread threatening to choke the life out of me. It was too much pressure. I wanted to help him, but he couldn't rely on me and only me. He had to rely on himself, too. I couldn't be all he had in his arsenal. "You need more than me. You need Dr. Montgomery, too."

"But I have you." He sat up, cupping my cheek. "Can't that be enough? I really think I'm getting better, Ginger. I don't need to talk to someone else to heal. I have you."

I shook my head, tears filling my eyes. Resting my palm on his heart, I soaked in the steady thumping against my palm. "I love you and I'm here for you, but I'm not enough."

"I'm fine." His arms tightened around me and his face lowered to mine. "Don't you see it in my eyes? I'm better. You're making me better."

I turned my face away, my heart wrenching so hard I thought I might collapse. Had he already forgotten about his fear at the door earlier? Did he truly believe he had it under control? Because he didn't. And neither did I.

I'd pulled him in closer, trusting our love to be strong enough to heal him. Trusting myself to know how to help him without overstepping my boundaries. By letting him back in, I might have made it worse.

So much worse.

chapter
eleven

Finn

The next morning, I stood by the bed and watched Carrie as she slept. She'd been shut behind the bedroom door all night long, but I'd snuck in to see her before she awoke. Carrie was curled up in the bed alone, her hand on the pillow beside her that she hugged to her chest. She used to rest her hand on my heart like that.

Now she had a fucking pillow instead of me.

I didn't dare move closer, because I didn't want to wake her up. Didn't want to break the moment. She'd hidden herself away from me last night after I'd mentioned that I felt I didn't need a therapist again. I shouldn't have said my thoughts out loud. She was so fucking convinced I needed help, but after I'd made love to her, I'd actually felt *normal* again.

I wish she could feel how I felt after she touched me. Then maybe she'd believe me when I said all I needed was her. She stirred and rubbed her nose, crinkling it up adorably, and glanced up at me within seconds. Her eyes were guarded. She sat up, holding the sheet to her chest. "Is everything okay?"

"Yeah, everything's fine," I said, smoothing her red hair off her face and tucking it behind her ear. "I'm going to grab some firewood and get some coffee started."

She nodded once. "Thanks."

"We'll talk when I get back in." I tipped her face up to mine and kissed her gently, brushing my thumb over her jawline. "I know that we need to talk."

She sat up, hugging her knees. "We do."

Heart in my throat, I walked out of the room. I made quick work of brushing my teeth, my mind on her words the whole time even as I walked out the front door. All she wanted was for me to agree to go talk to Dr. Montgomery a few hours a week. I might know I didn't need it, but *she* didn't. I might know this was only a small backslide, and that I'd be okay, but again, *she* didn't.

Could I do what she asked of me, while still knowing I wasn't actually admitting I needed her help to get better? While still making her see I was strong enough on my own? Was going to see Dr. Montgomery again really so much for her to ask at this point, after all I'd done?

I might not think I needed help, but *she* did. If she thought I needed help, then I'd get it for her. It wouldn't help, but I'd do it. It would help *her*.

Unlocking the front door, I stepped outside. As I headed toward the woodpile in nothing more than jeans and a pair of boots, I knew I'd finally come to the right conclusion. Knew my head was on straighter than it had been in a while. When I reached the spot where the wood was stored, I let out a relieved sigh. Once I'd agree to get help, she'd tell me to come home, and then we'd both be back to normal.

I could put this whole mess behind me.

As I bent down, I saw the tip of a bottle poking out from underneath the woodpile. I picked it up. Right away, I knew whose it was. It was her father's favorite scotch. His secret stash, I suppose. Or maybe it was something he'd just stored in the bottle for convenience purposes. Lighter fluid or some shit like that. I tossed the mostly full bottle back and forth between my hands, then cracked the lid and took a quick sniff.

Yep, definitely booze.

I stared down at it, my hands trembling, the old urge I'd avoided for so long hitting me like a fucking throat punch. For the first time in a long time, I wanted a drink. I felt like I needed a drink, and it was humbling. Maybe I didn't have my shit together quite as much as I'd liked to believe.

Closing my eyes, I focused on Carrie. On Susan. On putting that lid on that drink, but my fingers didn't move. I was immobilized. My hand lifted higher, and I finally realized it fully. I wasn't fine.

A few minutes later, I walked into the house, my arms filled with wood. When I opened the door, I tripped on the raised entrance and stumbled inside clumsily. "Smooth, Coram," I mumbled to myself.

Was it too much to hope that she hadn't seen my embarrassing entrance? I peeked over the wood. Of course it was. Carrie sat on the couch, her hands clasped tight in her lap. She looked like she was still in worry mode. "Grand entrance aside, I thought about it some more, and I—" I broke off mid-step, blinking at her. "What's wrong?"

She shook her head, not talking. She watched me with tears in her eyes. The way she looked at me...it reminded me of the way she'd looked at me the night she'd found me asleep on the couch.

"Stop it." My heart stuttered to a painful halt. "Why are you looking at me like that again?"

"Why, Finn?" Her beautiful red lips trembled and she just kind of broke. "Why did you do it to me again?"

I set the wood down, slowly, my eyes locked on hers. I was confused as hell. She was looking at me as if...as if she was done with me. It sent chills down my spine. "I have no idea what you're talking about right now. Are you okay?"

"No. I'm not." She crossed her arms, and her voice was so fucking hollow it was amazing I'd heard it at all. "But enough about me. Let's talk about you. Tell me, how was your drink?"

"My—?" I broke off, understanding hitting me like a knife to the fucking gut. She'd seen me out there with her father's scotch opened up and in my hands. "That wasn't mine. You have to believe me."

"No, I don't." She stood up, her fists rolled at her sides, and her cheeks wet with tears. "I looked out the window, because you were taking longer than usual, and you were out there with a freaking *drink* in your hand. You tricked me *again*. Lied to me *again*. Hid the truth from me *again*."

But I hadn't. Not this time. I stepped back, rage and pain making my vision red. "Are you fucking kidding me? You actually think I was out there at nine o'clock in the morning chugging back scotch? Is that really what you think of me?"

"You're seriously going to deny it?" She stomped her foot once. Actually stomped her foot. "I *saw* you, Finn!"

"You saw what you wanted to see, damn it," I snapped, tugging on the hair at the back of my head. "Again."

"What's that supposed to mean?"

"It means you're jumping to conclusions, like usual. It means you're unable to believe anything good about me anymore." I cupped the back of my neck, locking my hands and finally accepting this for what it was. "It means you don't have faith in me. Don't trust me. And never will. How can we possibly recover from that?"

She staggered back, her eyes wide. "Stop it. Stop turning this into something else. You need help, Finn. Turning to booze and pills and sex isn't going to give it to you."

"There it is again." I threw my hands up. "Those fucking words. 'You need help,'" I mimicked, making my voice high. "That's all you ever say to me anymore."

Something inside of her seemed to snap. That self-control and strength she'd had all weekend faded away, and I finally saw the hurt I'd caused her. Finally saw the pain deep within her. It shattered me. Fucking shattered me.

"That's because you *do*," she snarled.

"Maybe you do, too." I laughed a little uneasily. "Once upon a time, you would have seen a drink in my hand and believed me if I told you it wasn't mine. Once upon a time, you wouldn't have immediately assumed I was hiding something from you. Once upon a time, you would have trusted me."

"You broke that trust too many times," she whispered, fisting her hands at her sides. "That's on you, not *me*."

"Yeah, it's all on me. I know." I covered my face, dragging my hands down it. "I'm tired, Carrie. So fucking tired. I constantly have to prove myself, and even then? I fail."

She bit down on her lip, shaking her head slowly. "You had a bottle in your hand. Every time you've gone out there, it's been for a drink, hasn't it? For once in our whole relationship, just tell me the truth. Just admit it. You're self-medicating again."

"The only medication I wanted was *you*." I locked gazes with her. "And you just might fucking kill me instead of save me."

She swiped her hands across her cheeks. "You can't rely on me anymore. I can't do it. I'm not enough, again."

"You could be if you'd just believe me." I stared at her, willing her to actually see me. "Just believe in me, and I will be fine."

"How many times have you gotten a drink out of that bottle?"

"None." My shoulders drooped. "Not one fucking drop."

She shook her head sadly. She looked resigned, which scared the hell out of me. I'd only seen that look on her face one other time, and it had been right before we broke up. "I saw you. You had it in your hand. Have you gotten a drink every time you went outside? Was that whole thing an excuse?"

"Yes." I ground my teeth together. "Because I don't give a fuck about anything else but getting drunk. I certainly wasn't out there getting wood for the fire so we didn't freeze."

"Yeah, because that requires a drink," she said sarcastically.

"Lately, it fucking should." I stalked toward her. "I'm always making excuses, and I'm always fucking up. And you know what else?

Most of all, I'm tired of hurting you. I can't do it anymore. I won't."

Her eyes flashed fire at me. Blue, hot fire. "Oh, here we go again! We've done this before," she said. "Go on. Tell me I'm better off without you. Tell me you're leaving me so you can save me."

I swallowed hard past my swollen throat. "See? No matter what I do, or what I say, you're fucking pissed at me. Well, guess what? You win. I quit trying."

"Go ahead and quit." She shoved my shoulders. I stumbled back. "You've been dying to, haven't you? Dying to leave. Dying to be free and not answer to anyone anymore. That's why you keep doing this stuff, isn't it? So I kick you out and you don't have to feel bad for leaving. Well, go. Just *go*."

I stared at her, unable to believe she said those things. "*What?*"

"You heard me." She shoved my shoulders again, tears streaming down her wet cheeks. Her eyes looked bluer than the sky on a crystal clear summer day. "Go! I don't need you here, hiding things from me and lying to me. Making me think you're getting better when you're obviously not."

She was kicking me out again. Bullshit. I wasn't having it. "Actually, you do. I'm your ride."

"I'll call a taxi. That was something else I was used to doing *once upon a time*." She stormed past me, heading for the bedroom. I caught her elbow as she passed, knowing I should let her go, but unable to. "Let *go* of me. It hurts when you touch me." She broke off on a sob. "It hurts so freaking much."

It hurt me, too. But it would hurt even more if I let go. "If I told you I didn't drink anything, swore to you, would you believe me?"

"No." She yanked free, tears streaming down her face. "Not anymore."

My heart broke into a million pieces. I could tell her to smell my breath. I could prove to her I hadn't had a sip of that booze, that I'd been strong enough to put that bottle down, despite the desire to down it all in one swig. But in the end, it didn't matter what I'd done out there.

She didn't believe me, and never would again.

That was the real problem here.

"Then I fail to see how we can move past this." I needed her to be alive, but she didn't need me. Not anymore. "I will never be done loving you, damn it. Not even if you're with someone else, but I can't keep fighting the past. I can't keep letting you down."

She closed her eyes, not even bothering to wipe away the tears streaming down her cheeks anymore. "It's best if you go. We need to stop doing this. Need to stop torturing each other. This can't be love.

Not really."

"Agreed," I said, my voice cracking. "I love you, and I always will. Nothing you say or do will ever change that, and the fact that you don't know that is the number-one reason we'll never work. Correction: why we never worked."

She bit her lip. "That's not true. Don't take that from us. We were happy once."

"Yeah. Before…"

Hell, I didn't even know anymore. When had we stopped being happy?

"Since before Susan. Say it." She tossed her hair behind her back, her blue eyes shining with tears and so much pain that it hurt me to look at her. "You were on the fence in the first place, but now? You regret it. You regret her."

The fact that she believed that hurt. It really fucking hurt.

"No," I said, my voice hoarse. "I'd never regret one second of that baby girl, and I never will. What I regret is letting you forget how much you mean to me. I regret giving you a reason not to trust me. And I regret that you no longer love me. But I don't regret her, or you, or us. Never that."

She stared at me as if she didn't believe a word I said.

I didn't blame her.

History was repeating itself, and I couldn't fucking stop it. Nothing would. We were dying, and no one could save us. The best thing I could do for her would be to walk away again. It was all I was good at anymore. All I was ever good at.

And I needed to remember that.

chapter
twelve

Carrie

I watched him closely, wishing I could believe that he hadn't had a drink out there, but I was all out of blind faith today. I'd trusted and hoped and loved, and what had it gotten me? Lies. All lies. That's all he'd ever given me, it seemed.

God, I was so tired of trying to uncover the truth. So tired of wondering when he'd ever be honest with me. Was this really what was best for our children?

Us never really believing one another?

Shaking my head, I pressed my hands to my stomach. "It's not too late. You can still get help," I said, refusing to give up on him. Even if we weren't together, even if he left me, he had to be okay. I had to know he was okay. "Please, Finn. Think of Susan."

He shook his head; his eyes filled with unshed tears. "Don't do that. Don't use her against me. That's not fair."

"She needs you, Finn. She needs her father in her life." I took a step toward him, stumbling a little. "Don't you want to walk her down the aisle? Teach her how to love? How to have fun? How to *trust*?"

"Stop," Finn said, his face going red. His fingers quivered as he tugged on his hair. "I can't do this. Not anymore. I can't do this."

He kept repeating those words, over and over again. Trembling, he covered his face and turned from me. It broke my heart to see him like this. I wanted to help him so badly, but all I kept doing was making it worse. He had to do this for himself. Not for me.

I took a step toward him. "I'm sorry. Sorry I yelled. Let me—"

I pressed a hand to my stomach. I felt like...like...

Crap. I was going to be sick.

I ran for the bathroom, one hand to my stomach and the other pressed to my mouth. As soon as I hit the floor on my knees, my stomach violently expelled what little food I had in it. Finn came up behind me, close but not too close. I knew that he got sick when he was around other people who were sick, so I was surprised he'd followed me at all. He hovered behind me, cursed, and squatted next to me.

Gently, he swooped my hair off my face and held it in his fist. "Shit, Carrie. Are you okay?"

I nodded, gripping the edges of the toilet so hard it hurt, but I didn't speak.

"Are you done?"

Again, I nodded.

He swept my hair away from the danger zone and braided it. I swallowed, memories hitting me hard and fast. He'd learned how to braid when I'd been pregnant with Susan. He used to brush it for me before braiding it, claiming he needed the practice before his princess came along.

It had soothed me back then. The effect was quite opposite this time. This time, it made me want to cry. After he grabbed a ponytail holder off the sink and secured the braid, he tenderly rested the braid against my back.

"I'll get you a washcloth."

I didn't nod or move this time. I was too busy listening to the thudding of my heart. I hadn't puked since the first trimester with Susan. And before that, it had been years. All the way back when I'd been in college, and Finn and I had been fighting. He'd nursed me back to health back then.

He was doing it again now.

Would he start asking questions? Would he put two and two together and realize why I'd been so emotional lately? I was so terrified that in the face of all our fighting and heartbreak, that the news would make him break even more.

He came back, his eyes locked on me. He bent down beside me again, peeled me off the toilet, and closed the lid. With a flick of his hand, it flushed. Slowly, he wiped the washcloth over my forehead, cheeks, and mouth.

I closed my eyes, swallowing past the lump in my throat. "Thank you."

He tossed the washcloth in the tub and rocked back on his heels. I opened my eyes, and he was there, looking pale, sweaty, but as loyal as always. "Anytime, anywhere."

Swallowing past my throbbing throat, I struggled to my feet, but he beat me to it and helped me up. Once I stood straight, he let go of me and stepped back, swiping a hand down his face. "Finn, we need to—"

At the same time, Finn said, "You got yourself so worked up, you—"

The front door opened, and we both froze. Finn stiffened and looked at me with horror on his face, but he quickly sprang into action. "Stay in here. Do *not* leave."

He slammed the door in my face. For a second, I stood there, unable to process what had just happened, but I snapped myself into reality and followed him. I yanked the bathroom door open, my heart pounding so hard it hit my ribs, and bolted into the room.

When I saw what had caused the disturbance, I froze.

Dad stood in the doorway. "Everything is fine now. They caught the guy lurking around the woods today, about a mile from here, and he's in holding right now." I blinked, listening to my dad's voice, unable to process it. "Does Carrie know about the threat? Did you tell her about it?"

"No. I didn't tell her about him. I can't believe he was so close and I didn't know it." Finn tugged on the hair at the back of his head. His nervous tic. "You had guys watching this place?"

"Of course I did." My father shrugged. "As you pointed out, if Carrie is in danger, I'd put a whole team on her. So I did."

"But you said he wasn't a real—"

I gripped the doorjamb tight because the world was spinning all around me. They were talking about a bad guy having been caught, and Dad was asking Finn if he'd told me about it, and I was scared to death that Finn had lied to me again. For the millionth time.

"Who got caught?" I asked, my voice breaking. "What are you guys talking about?"

Finn looked at me, his face pale.

"Hey, Princess." Dad stepped inside the living room, shutting the door behind him. "There was a guy who threatened you, but it wasn't a big deal. I told Finn about it, and also about my plan to get you out here so we could get the guy while you were safely tucked away out of reach. I mean, he wasn't a huge threat in the first place, but—"

"I was in danger." I didn't even look at him. My attention was focused squarely on my husband. "You were guarding me again, and you didn't tell me?"

He paled even more. "I wasn't. He wasn't a huge threat."

"But he was a threat." I gripped the doorjamb even tighter. "You knew I was in danger, you brought me out here, and you didn't tell me?"

"Yes. No. Maybe. I don't know, damn it. I don't know anything anymore." He stepped closer. "I knew about it, but I also knew that he wasn't a threat. Not really. Your dad told me as much."

"I did. He wasn't a big threat at all," Dad agreed. "He's right."

It didn't matter. Finn had lied to me about the drugs. He'd lied to me about the drinking. And he'd lied to me when I'd asked him if there was a reason he was acting so worried about every single noise.

He'd lied to me so much I didn't know what was real anymore. I didn't know if any of it was real anymore.

"It's over," Finn said, his voice so soft I barely heard him. "You're safe now."

I swallowed hard, blinking back tears, and shook my head. "I was never safe. Not really."

Finn stared at me, his pain clear in his face.

It made me wonder if mine was, too.

"What's going on?" Dad looked back and forth. "Did you two work everything out while you were here?"

"There's no danger, no matter how small it might be, anymore, right?" Finn asked, his voice breaking. "She's safe now?"

Dad flushed. "Yes. He's been apprehended. But there's obviously something going on here, and you two need to fix this for Susan before you leave."

I closed my eyes. I wanted to. I really did. But he didn't. He refused to admit he needed help, and there was nothing I could do with that. He needed to want to save himself, and he didn't want to. Not yet anyway. He wasn't ready.

And I couldn't save him if he didn't save himself.

It was time to think of Susan's safety. That, and the little one growing inside of my belly. I had to put them first this time. I had to give up. I knew what was coming, and it hurt.

Finn grabbed his bag off the couch. My heart fell to my feet, all bloody and torn into shreds. "Sir, can you excuse us?" Finn asked, his knuckles white on his bag.

Dad looked back and forth between us, his face going paler by the second. "No. You two can't do this. Don't give up on each other."

I had no idea how my dad had even known we'd been fighting in the first place, but I wasn't about to ask. Not when Finn had one foot out the door. Not when everything was falling apart, one step at a time. Not when I was about to lose him.

"Dad. Please." I finally tore my gaze off of Finn and looked at him. "Go wait outside. We need a minute."

Dad left, his shoulders hunched. It was almost kind of funny that after years of him hating Finn and me together, back when we'd been dating, now he was championing Finn. Trying to fix our issues.

And *I* was the one who had to push Finn away so he could get the help he needed. How had it come to this again? Why was I never enough to make him better?

Finn gripped the straps of his bag even harder. "After all we've been through, after how hard I've tried, you'll always think the worst of me. Every time. That's how much I fucked us up, and that's not something that can be fixed."

"I'm sorry," I whispered, curling my hands into fists. I wanted to tell him to forget everything, to come home with me. But that wouldn't help him. It wouldn't make him better. I was toxic for him, and nothing I did or said would change that. "I'm so, so sorry."

He nodded, not meeting my eyes. "I know. I am too."

"Can't we—?"

"No. We need to stop." He let out a shuddering breath. "You don't trust me. You were right. We have to stop torturing each other. Stop hurting each other. It's time to stop fighting the world together. It's time to stop fighting to be together when we're clearly not meant to be. It's over, Carrie. It's been over, but we didn't even know it."

"How can you say that?" I hugged my arms to my chest, tears slipping out of my eyes for what felt like the millionth time this weekend. "It's not true."

"But it is." He walked up to me and cupped my face, gently wiping the tears away with both thumbs. "I love you more than life itself, and at times, I think I've always loved you more than you loved me."

I shook my head frantically. "That's not true at all."

"But it is." He smiled sadly. "And that was okay, because I didn't care that we were lopsided. But this time, I care. I need…we need…love isn't always enough. It isn't always going to save everything. We have to…we have to give up, Ginger. We have to stop fighting the world, and we have to start fighting for ourselves. It's time."

A sob escaped me, and I covered my mouth. My ribs closed in on my lungs, making it impossible to breathe. I *couldn't* breathe. Couldn't think. Couldn't *live*. Not if he was leaving me. Not if he was giving up on me.

Not if he actually thought he'd always loved me more than I loved him.

It wasn't true. None of it was.

"I can't. I can't, not without you. You can get the help you need, and then you can come home to us." I gripped his arms tight, refusing to let go. In the face of losing him forever, I knew I couldn't let him leave. "You can be with us again."

He shook his head. "This isn't just because of the pills or the PTSD. It's the lies. I've told so many lies, and you don't trust me anymore. You never will. It's over. I ruined it. That's why I'm leaving."

But I wanted him to stay. I wanted to grow old together, the two of us, and raise our kids together. Live, laugh, and love together. "*Please. Please* don't do this."

He dropped his forehead to mine, his own breathing shaky and rough sounding. "Shit, Ginger, I don't want to, but I have to. I have to do it for you."

He pressed his mouth to mine, kissing me sweetly one last time, and then let go of me. As he headed for the door, I pressed a hand to my stomach and bit down on my tongue. I could tell him about the baby right now, and he'd come back. He'd come back and stay. I knew he would.

But I wouldn't do that to him.

If he came back, it had to be because he wanted to. After he got help, he had to *want* to come back to me. Not because he'd been forced to by my news.

I'd tell him, but not like this. Not now.

"I love you," I said, my voice so soft I wasn't sure he'd hear it at all. "I love you so much, Finn."

He froze in the doorway, his head dropping. We hadn't said that to each other lately. Not really. It had all been almost…mechanic. As if we simply told each other where we needed to be and when, and that was what our marriage had become.

And now, it was over.

Because he walked out the door.

I collapsed to the floor, hand to my heart, and burst into bone-shattering, uncontrollable, heartbreaking tears. I didn't think I'd ever stop. Because he…he…

He actually gave up.

chapter thirteen

Finn

I sat on the hotel bed, staring blankly at the door. Nothing moved. Nothing made me flinch. Nothing made me smile. There was nothing inside of me but an aching loneliness and the knowledge that if I died today, no one would give a damn anymore. I was on my own, and it was my fault.

I just sat there, staring at nothing and everything, feeling empty inside. It had been this way all week long, since I'd walked away from Carrie, and it would be this way forever.

I'd sworn to love her forever, and damn it, I would. But in this case, I'd loved her enough to know she needed me to go. I'd done it once before. It had almost killed me.

And now, I was doing it again.

This time, she'd been making herself physically ill. She'd gotten sick, all because she was so worked up over me, and her, and our fight. I'd physically made her ill.

How fucked up was that?

It wasn't fair to her. I was dark and twisted and fucked up. A man Carrie didn't need in her life. I wasn't healthy. I wasn't the man she needed. So I'd let go.

And I'd been right. It had hurt like hell.

The clock switched to five with a flash, and I slowly stood. It was time to go see Susan for my visitation, and that meant it was time to see Carrie again for the first time since I'd walked away. Since I'd given up on us. We worked on the same military base, but I'd managed to avoid her for the most part.

A lot of that was probably because she was avoiding me, too. I was so damn empty inside. So damn lonely. Maybe being with my baby girl would help.

I missed her like hell, and her smile never ceased to get to me. Never ceased to make me smile, and it had been way too fucking long since I smiled. Since that one night in the cabin with Carrie. And even then, it had felt surreal. As if I'd been walking on a land mine, and it had been about to explode.

Frowning in the mirror, I smoothed my button-up shirt over my stomach and swiped my palms down the thighs of my ripped blue jeans. I'd been alone for way too long now, but I hadn't had a drop of booze in me. Hadn't taken a single pill.

Hadn't even wanted to.

Someone knocked on the door, and I jerked to attention, my palms sweating and my heart pounding in my ears so loudly it hurt my head. It drowned out the voices screaming for help. And the fear...fuck, the fear. I was so sick of being afraid.

So sick of myself, too.

"Who is it?" I called out.

"Service desk, sir," a male voice that sounded somewhat familiar called out. "We have a message for you."

I walked to the door slowly, taking calming breaths as I made my way across the room. It was just a knock. Nothing more. Nothing less. *One. Two. Three.* The voices quieted down with each breath I took. *Four.* After I unlatched the chain, I opened the door slowly.

When I saw who stood there, I almost shut it in his face. Not because I wasn't happy to see him, because I was. But because he'd see how fucking lost I was right now. "She call you?"

Riley, an old college friend of Carrie's and mine, rocked back on his heels. "Did who call me?"

I rolled my eyes. "Quit the innocent act. There's only one person who knows where I am staying, and she has red hair."

"Okay. You got me." Riley grinned. He still had the same blond hair and green eyes as before, but he was no longer the college kid he'd been when I met him. He was all grown up...as much as he'd ever be, anyway. "Can I come in?"

"I have to leave." Despite my words, I opened the door and let him inside. "I'm supposed to go see Susan tonight."

"It's fine. Carrie's running late, anyway, because she was with me."

I stiffened, despite my trust in both him and Carrie. Riley had always had a thing for her, and something told me despite the life he now lived…that *thing* had never really died. "Jumping in already? My side of the bed isn't even cold yet."

"I'm engaged, dude." Riley brushed past me. "Calm your jealous hormones—though it's good to see you still care. She thinks you don't."

"One of the many problems our relationship has."

"The biggest one is the fact that you left and haven't contacted her, besides to shoot her a text that you'd be visiting Susan on Friday." Riley crossed his arms. "What the fuck, man?"

My cheeks heated. "I assure you there's more to the story than that."

"Oh, I think I know most of it. More than you do, even." He hesitated, and dropped his arms to his sides. "She came to me for legal advice, man. Asking for help in case it came to…"

"Legal advice?" My heart stuttered. I closed my eyes. "Not…*oh*."

Of course. She was moving forward. Without me.

I'd told her to, after all.

"Yes. That. The big 'D' word. She isn't looking into it yet, but she thinks it's what you want. Thinks you're done for good." Riley crossed the room and stopped in front of me. "You need to get your shit together, go over there, and fix this. Now."

Divorce. Carrie was actually looking into the possibility of divorce. I staggered back as if Riley had physically hit me, and I almost wished he had. It would have hurt less than this. The reality of what was happening to me, of all that I was losing, hit me like an iron anvil on the head.

I'd known it was coming, but it didn't make it hurt any less.

"*Fuuuck*," I snarled, heading for the door.

The ever-present rage sent my blood coursing through my veins at breakneck speeds. And pain. So much fucking pain that it nearly blinded me.

Nearly incapacitated me. It might still.

"Hey, hey," Riley said, jumping in front of me. "You need to calm down, man. Didn't you tell her it's what you wanted?"

"I don't *want* this. How could I ever fucking *want* this?" I pushed him out of the way. "And I can't be *calm*."

"Yeah." Riley shoved me back. "You fucking can."

My eyes narrowed on him. "Did you just fucking *push* me?"

"Yeah. But you pushed me first." He shoved my shoulders even harder. "And I'll do it again, too, if it's what I need to do to get you to use your head."

"You want me to use my head?"

"Yes, I do." He eyed me cautiously. "Think things through for once in your life."

Snarling, I took a swing at him, not even stopping to think it through. Not even bothering to remember that this was my friend, and that he was trying to help me. Trying to help *us*. I just reacted. "Fuck you."

"Dude." Riley leapt back, his eyes wide. He stumbled back, his hands up in the air. "Finn, *stop* it."

I stalked toward him. "Give me one good reason not to kick your ass right now."

"Susan. I'm her godfather." He cocked his head. "Is that good enough?"

Mid-step, I froze. Slowly, I uncurled my fists, cracked my knuckles, and fisted them again. "Damn you."

"I get that you're confused, hurt, angry, and feeling bloodthirsty right now. I do." Riley dropped his hands; his green eyes locked on mine with way too much compassion. "But you can't mess this thing up again. You guys have to work this out. You just have to."

I shook my head, trying to clear it. The word "divorce" was ringing in it nonstop. It was such a dirty fucking word. One I'd never thought I'd have to speak in the same sentence as Carrie's name. "Why do you care so much?"

"Because if you two can't make it work, there's no hope for the rest of us." He rubbed the back of his neck. "If you two are getting divorced, then I'm screwed before I even get married. I've never seen anyone in love as much as the two of you. Ever."

"Not even you and—"

"No." Riley lifted a shoulder. "Not even close, man."

I wanted to revisit that, but at another time. "I don't know if it can be fixed this time," I said, rubbing my temples. "The things she used to love about me? She now hates. The spontaneous nature she once used to go crazy for? Now she yells at me for not planning things through. And the lies. So many lies..."

Riley stared at me. "People grow up. They change. You just have to try to change together."

"Don't you think I'm fucking trying? Huh?" My chest tightened. "I don't know why I flipped out, really. It's what I told her to do. Move on. Try again with someone who's more like her. We've tried hard enough, and we've failed."

"Bullshit," Riley snapped. "Shut the fuck up."

"We just don't work," I said. "As much as I hate it, it's true. We're not a good couple at all. She'd be happier with someone from your world."

I eyed him. I'd once thought he and Carrie would make the perfect couple, and it was true. They would. They were the same. I was...*me*. I'd thought we could move past that, but I don't think we could. I think it's why we were here, on the brink of divorce.

Riley stiffened. "Don't even think about looking at me like that. You're the perfect guy for her. Not me."

I shrugged like I didn't give a damn when I clearly did. "Whatever, man."

"Plus, I'm engaged."

"And I'm married," I mumbled, staring down at my platinum wedding ring. "Shit changes in the blink of an eye. It's called life."

"Why did you do it?" Riley watched me closely. Too closely. "Why did you take those pills again? And why didn't you tell her the truth? You know how much she hates lies. You had to know it would end this way."

"I didn't think at all," I admitted. "I couldn't."

"Why not?"

"I was in pain, and I was in hell again. The accident brought me back to...to what I was when we met. A big fucking mess." I averted my eyes, my cheeks growing hot. "Nightmares. Panic attacks. Migraines. You name it, I had it. I thought if I could at least take the pain away, I could maybe handle the rest. I was wrong."

"But why didn't you tell her?" he asked, his voice soft. "She could have helped you."

I squared my jaw. "I was worried we'd break up again. We did."

"*After* she caught you in a bunch of lies. If you'd been straightforward with her, maybe it would have ended differently. Did you tell her that you were suffering from PTSD again?" he asked.

"Yes." I shoved my hands in my pockets. "After."

"Are you seeing a therapist again?"

"No." I headed for the door. "I'll be fine on my own."

Riley clenched his jaw and stepped in my path again. "But what if you aren't?"

"Then I'm not." I flexed my fingers. "But it doesn't change the fact that we've been destroyed by my actions and lies. There's no fixing that."

"What are you going to do about Carrie, then?" Riley followed me. "Just roll over and let her leave you? Let her move on? Marry another man? Let another man raise your child? Watch as another man fucks your wi—?"

I slammed him into the wall, bunching his shirt in my fist and exerting enough pressure on his chest to make him stop talking. "Shut your fucking mouth."

"What?" He grinned at me cockily, looking entirely unconcerned that an unstable Marine with PTSD was seconds from killing him. "It's what will happen if you let her go. Did you think she'd become a nun?"

"I didn't—" I broke off, shoving him a little harder against the wall. "I didn't think about it at all. Not really. We're supposed to be spending the rest of our lives together. Now we're not, and it hurts so much I don't really see much point in doing anything anymore. It's all just an act of moving from one thing to the next. There's no future. No anything. That's all I know."

My voice cracked on the last word, but I didn't even bother to act embarrassed. That's how awful the thought of not growing old with Carrie felt. It was worse than an IED explosion, or a car accident that barely managed to total my car…

But managed to total my life.

chapter
fourteen

Carrie

At ten after five, I stared at myself in the mirror for a second. I'd
put on a little bit of red lipstick, a dress, and Finn's favorite pair
of black boots. The ones he said belonged over my head instead of
on the floor. We hadn't spoken or even seen each other ever since he'd
walked away from me.

I missed him *so* freaking much. I'd spent the whole week crying,
tossing and turning, and trying to stay strong for him. Trying to realize
that leaving was just something he had to do to get better, and I had to
accept that. He was trying to get better, but he needed to do it alone. I
had to believe that when he was ready, he'd come back.

For a split second earlier today, I'd doubted that.

I'd doubted that love would be enough for us. I'd even had a late
lunch with Riley and sought his advice on divorce in case it became
necessary. But just saying the word had made me realize it wouldn't
be. I had to have faith in us. In our love.

He'd come home when he was ready.

He was coming to visit Susan tonight. She was upstairs taking
her late afternoon nap, but she'd be awake any second now. Since I
knew he'd be hanging out for a while, I'd cooked his favorite meal
for him. Usually he did the cooking, but every once in a while I made

homemade fettuccine Alfredo, and he begged for it.

I was hoping he'd take it as the sign it was. A sign of my belief that he'd get better, and he'd come home. My phone rang, and I glanced down at it. It was my dad. He'd called like ten times in the past hour, but I'd been ignoring it so I could get ready.

The doorbell rang at the same time as the phone. I silenced the ringer, not wanting my talk with Finn to be interrupted, took a steady breath, and opened the door.

I started talking before I even saw him. "She's still asleep, but she'll be up any—" I broke off. It wasn't Finn. It was a man I'd never seen before. He had a black hat on, a black hoodie, and his hands were behind his back. He looked like a deliveryman or something. "I'm sorry. I thought you were someone else. Can I help you?"

"Yeah. You can. I didn't want to do this, you know."

My heart sped up. This man…something wasn't right. "Didn't want to do what?"

"Hurt anyone." The man lifted a shaking hand. It took me a second, but then I saw it. There was a gun in his hand. He shoved me through the open door of my home, and I stumbled backward. "But he's left me no choice. None at all."

I kept one hand behind my back, trying to keep my calm. Trying not to panic, but it was kind of hard when a man you didn't know was holding a gun with a shaky hand that was pointed at your face. "No one needs to get hurt, sir. What's wrong? Who didn't leave you a choice?"

"Him. Your father." The man scratched his temple with the gun, letting out a terrifying sob. With his free hand, he reached into his pocket and shoved a bunch of photos at me. "*Look* at them."

I took them with trembling hands. A young woman with blonde hair smiled at the camera. "Is this…?" My voice cracked because it was hard to talk. The fear he'd brought out in me was debilitating. My knees were trembling and I'd broken out in a sweat. All I could think was that my own daughter was upstairs asleep, and I had to keep her safe from this madman. "Is this your daughter?"

"Yes." He scratched his temple with the gun again, and snatched the photos back. He shoved them into his pocket. "Someone took her life with a gun, and now I'm going to do it to you. To *his* daughter."

I held one hand out, a small cry escaping me when he whipped the gun back toward me. My thumb flew over my phone, behind my back. "Who are you? Let me help you, please. Let me help you. I can help."

"There's only one way you can help me." He gave me an evil grin. The kind that sent shivers down your spine because you knew the person giving it to you was dangerous. "Y-Y-Y-You can die."

It seemed as if time was frozen, or suspended, or something. As if in slow motion, my brain realized three things. One: This man was going to kill me in my own house. Two: Susan was going to cry when he shot me. Three: Finn was going to find me dead.

He'd already seen enough death in his lifetime.

This would kill him.

But if he got here in time, he could stop it. He could save me again. He had to be close to the house by now. And I had to let him know there was danger. He couldn't just walk in, unaware of the situation. He could get hurt.

"Wait. No, please." I backed up, a hand held up in the air, and the man followed me. I hit the last button of Finn's phone number. With a trembling hand, I hit dial. "Who are you? Why are you doing this?"

"My name's Kyle Farmer. But it doesn't matter." The man smiled evilly, and a sickening shudder went up my spine and through my body. "Because you're going to be dead."

My heart thudded so fast and hard it hurt, and all I could hear was what might possibly be the last beats my heart ever made. I knew that name. It was the name of the man my father had said threatened me—and then he'd said hadn't been a real threat.

If that was true, then why was he here?

I swallowed hard. "Please. Take what you want, but please don't hurt me."

"But you see…" The man cocked the gun. "What I want is your life."

He said it so calmly, so clearly enunciated, that I *knew* he meant it. Over the years, I'd worked with a lot of different types of people. I'd seen lots of severely ill and disturbed people. And I'd treated people who were off their meds and had a chemical imbalance, as well as people who were just sad and needed to talk.

But this guy? He was the worst kind.

He was the type of guy who would kill an entire family without flinching, and not even feel a single moment of remorse over it. "Please," I whispered.

Was Finn on the phone? Was he hearing any of this?

Headlights hit the front door, and I closed my eyes in relief. Finn was here. He'd save me, like he always did. But he'd need my help if he was going to do it safely and—

A loud boom reverberated through the house, and the next thing I knew…

The world went black.

And everything ceased to exist.

Finn

I drove down the road that led to Carrie's driveway at twelve after five, slowing down as I approached. My heart pounded fast and hard as I did so. From the road, I could see all the lights downstairs were on, but the upstairs was dark. That was the first thing I noticed. The second thing I noticed was the wide open door, which struck me as odd.

Carrie didn't usually open the door before I came over...

I stopped on the side of the road, not sure how to proceed. Did she have company? Then I saw it. A motorcycle hidden in the shadows. Carrie wasn't alone. But who would she have here when she knew I was—?

My phone rang, and I picked it up, staring at the open door the whole time. "Hello?"

There was no one there.

"Hello?" I said again, my eyes still on the door. I pulled the phone back and stared at it. Carrie. But why was she calling me? And why couldn't I hear her? I put the phone back to my ear. "I'm outside on the road. Why are you calling me?"

No reply.

I listened closely. I could barely make it out, but I heard something about guns...and... "Please. Take what you want, but please don't hurt me."

Shit. Someone was in there, and he was trying to hurt my Carrie.

Cursing under my breath, I peeled into the driveway and threw my door open. As soon as my foot hit the driveway, a loud bang broke the silence of the night, and for a split second, I was frozen. Ever since the IED explosion, loud noises sent me flying backward, looking for cover. But this time I knew she needed me.

I couldn't afford to panic.

Couldn't listen to the voices in my head.

Carrie had taken one of my guns, but she hadn't taken the second one. I yanked my Glock out of my holster and bolted the rest of the way to the door, my heart thundering and my legs feeling weak as hell, yet stronger than ever.

Because inside that house was my family.

A man dressed all in black came out the door, a silver revolver in his hand. When he saw me, he startled and lifted his arm, the gun pointed at my chest. I reacted without thinking. Didn't let myself think. I just pulled the trigger.

Another deafening boom, and then he hit the ground without taking a shot. My hurried aim had been good, because I got him square between the eyes. There was no doubt in my mind that he was dead.

Even so, I crept closer and kicked the gun out of his reach.

The cops would want that later.

Neighbors were screaming and people were shouting in suburbia panic, but I didn't really hear them. I just stared at the man on my front porch and watched as the blood poured out of his head, staining my white concrete. I'd killed a man, after years of being tortured by the memories of my dying platoon.

Now he'd haunt me too. This man.

But then I remembered why he'd been there in the first place. "Carrie," I whispered, my chest going tight. "*Carrie!*"

I leapt over the dead body, and the sightless brown eyes, and skidded into the foyer of my house. The house Carrie and I had built together, after months of planning and plotting. I'd just killed a man on the front porch. We hadn't planned for that.

When I ran into the house, I slipped and fell, banging my head hard on the floor. Blinking, I rolled over onto all fours and looked down at what I'd slipped on. My vision was blurry and twisted, but what I'd fallen on was red and thick and...

"Oh, God. No. No, no, no, no, no."

There was blood on the marble floor, and it wasn't from the man I'd shot. Which meant it had to belong to...*no.*

I followed the trail of blood.

High-heeled black boots that I recognized instantly, because they were my favorite. A short black dress that hugged curves perfectly, which was also my favorite. And I could smell my favorite dinner cooking in the kitchen, as well as my favorite dessert.

Long red hair was splayed across the cold floor, a stark contrast to the tan marble beneath it, and then blood... So much fucking blood.

I choked on the smell. On the fear.

Reality blurred with the past, until I wasn't sure what was real and what wasn't. Not anymore. Maybe not ever again.

I stumbled forward on my hands and knees, the Glock I'd still been holding hitting the floor with a bang. I heard people come up behind me, crying out, but I didn't even look at them. I couldn't look away from my beautiful, porcelain, pale, motionless wife. "No. No, no, no, no. Carrie, *no.*"

I'd seen a lot of men like this. Watched a lot of people die. But I'd never expected to find her like this. Never expected to find her like this.

Never...

"Oh my God," someone said behind me. "Is she...?"

"No, no, no, no, no," I repeated. "This isn't real. This can't be real. It's a nightmare. It has to be a nightmare. Wake up. Wake up. Wake up." I punched my thigh as hard as I could. I didn't wake up. "*Carrie. Wake up.*"

I knelt next to her, soaking my pants with her blood, and reached out with a shaky hand. It was covered in blood—I had no idea whose—and rested my hand on her throat. This couldn't be how it ended. This couldn't be how *we* ended. I choked on a sob, burning tears streaming down my face, and pressed my fingers to her neck, where her pulse should be.

Nothing. I felt nothing.

"*Please God, let it be there. Let her be alive. I need her to be alive. Is she alive?*"

"I don't know," someone said, resting his hand on my shoulder. I hadn't realized I said anything out loud. "We called 911, but is there a pulse? They want to know..."

I shook my head, unable to stop. "No. Not Carrie. It can't be real. *This isn't real.*"

Susan cried from upstairs. My neighbor, the woman who I'd waved to earlier in the week, stepped forward. "I'll get her, but I won't bring her down."

I didn't answer. I couldn't.

Because I was realizing this wasn't a dream.

And I had to pull my shit together and save my wife.

I stared at the gaping wound on her head. He'd shot her. Aimed for her head and shot her in cold blood. I wished I could kill him again, endlessly, to make him suffer. I closed my eyes and forced myself to concentrate on the skin under my fingertips. And then there it was. Faint, but steady.

A heartbeat.

"She's alive," I rasped, crawling closer and glancing at the man on the phone. "She's not dead."

Hovering over her body, I pressed my fingers against the wound that gushed blood from her chest. She had two injuries. How was that even possible? There had been only one shot. I was sure of it. "She's bleeding from two wounds," I managed to say. "Not one."

The man behind me, a neighbor whose name I couldn't remember, told the operator what I'd said, word for word. Then he asked, "Are they both gunshot wounds?"

I scanned the foyer, forcing my eyes off of her. The table by the door was broken, and the glass vase I'd bought her for our first anniversary was shattered across the floor in millions of fragments. I turned her head to the side and ripped my shirt off.

The majority of the blood came from the wound on her chest, but the blood on her head seemed to be from something besides a gunshot wound. I pressed a trembling hand to the wound above her heart, trying to stop the blood. "No. She was shot in the chest, and it looks like she hit her head falling down. But it's bad. Really, really bad."

Tears fell from my cheeks, but I didn't bother to wipe them away.

"Carrie? God, Carrie, can you hear me? Don't leave me. Don't you dare fucking leave me." I lowered my head, closed my eyes, and kissed her. She felt cold, but not dead. Still, but not lifeless. "You can't leave me. I need you, Ginger."

She didn't even so much as lift a finger.

Sirens sounded in the distant background, and tires squealed directly outside the house, crashing into something. My truck, maybe.

"No! Carrie!" her father shouted, his voice frantic. "*Carrie!*"

I hugged her close, my hand still pressed to her chest. A scuffle came from behind me, and I closed my eyes. "Let him in. He's family."

My father-in-law came up behind me and froze. I knew the second he saw his lifeless daughter on the ground, because he fell to his knees. Just like I had. "*No.*"

"She's not dead." I looked over my shoulder at him. He looked ashen, and his eyes were locked on Carrie's lifeless face. "Hey! Look at me." He did. "She's not gone," I said, stating each word perfectly.

"Susan?"

"Is fine," I managed to say. "She wasn't hurt."

He collapsed upon himself. "This is all my fault. I did this to her. This is my fault."

"If anything, it's mine. I should have been there with her. I should have been here." I'd failed her, because I'd been too worried about taking care of myself. I'd left her alone, and now this had happened. I looked down at her again, my heart twisting harshly. "I did this. I should have been here. It's my fault."

He reached out and clasped her hand. "That man out there? He's the man who was a threat last week. He got out. He escaped custody. This is my fault. All my fault…"

I stiffened, the blood rushing out of my head. "*What?*"

"It's him. This is my fault." He fell back on his butt, his eyes still locked on Carrie. "This is all my fault. We didn't know…I didn't realize…"

My grip on my shirt, which was still pressed to her bleeding chest, tightened so hard it hurt. The cotton actually hurt my fingers. "That son of a—"

Sirens sounded, and Carrie started to tremble, then shake.

And then she seized.

chapter
fifteen

Carrie

I woke up slowly, blinking my eyes a few times before finally opening them to the glaring light overhead. Everything hurt. Breathing. Opening my eyes. Blinking. So, I closed them again, a small moan escaping me. Someone grabbed my hand, the touch gentle and reassuring. It soothed me instantly.

"Carrie?" a male voice asked. "Are you awake?"

Carrie? Who was Carrie? Was that me?

Why couldn't I remember?

"I'm here, Ginger. I'm with you." The man kissed my hand, his grip firm yet gentle. "I'm not going anywhere."

Ginger? I thought he'd called me Carrie. I was so confused. So high, in so much pain, and so confused. So…*everything*. Slowly, I opened my eyes and blinked again, the bright light sending a shaft of pain piercing through my throbbing skull.

Turning my head to the side, I opened my eyes again, and focused on the man beside me. He had light brown—or was it dark blond?—hair, stunning blue eyes, and he was simply too gorgeous for words.

My first thought was that this was the type of guy fathers hated. Sexy. Dangerous. Sexy. Trouble. *Sexy*. Even so, when I locked eyes with him, I knew he was so much more than that. And I also sensed that he was someone important to me. I *knew* I knew him, straight down to my very soul, even if I couldn't remember who the heck he was. My heartbeat picked up rapidly, and my fingers flexed on his.

Somehow, I knew this man...

When he saw my eyes had opened, he smiled at me, bright and wide, and I blinked again. He was even more handsome when he smiled. That smile...it did weird things to my insides. It made me think of...of...

God, I couldn't remember.

"Carrie?" He offered me a small smile. "Hey. It's me. I hope you don't mind I stayed. I had to be here when you woke up."

I glanced away, but turned back instantly, almost as if I couldn't stop looking at him. As if my eyes were on some sort of magnetic connection with his, and it was inevitable for me to fight it. To try to look away. "Do I know...? Who are you?"

He stared at me, and the smile slowly faded away. "What? It's me."

I let go of him, hugging my hand to my chest defensively. Something about him, the way he looked at me...it hurt. It physically hurt. "I don't know you. Who are you? Who am I?"

"Carrie..." His voice broke, and he reached for my hand again. I snatched it out of reach. "Don't you remember me? It's Finn."

It was as if that name held magical powers or something, because as soon as he said it, everything came rushing back. It all came back in a horrifying, painful, way-too-graphic rush. The fear, when that man had pointed his gun at me. The pain, after he'd shot. The horrifying blackness when I'd been sure I was going to die...

I sucked in a deep breath, but it got stuck. I couldn't breathe.

I was choking on my own blood all over again.

"Shh. Just breathe. You're okay. You can do it. Just breathe." Finn grabbed me and hugged me close, his touch gentle. "It's okay. I'm here with you."

I let my breath out in a whoosh and clung to him with the arm that didn't hurt like hell. I'd been shot. I'd been attacked in my own home, and I'd...oh my God. I pulled back, my eyes wide. "*Susan.*"

"She's okay." He met my eyes. "She's safe. He didn't get her."

I shook my head, tears filling my eyes. Sadness and fear and pain. So much pain. Susan was okay, but what about the other one? The one who'd been in my belly? He or she had to be okay, too. Please, God. "O-Our baby? Is our baby okay, too?"

Finn blinked at me, looking confused for a second. Then he nodded. "Everything is fine."

I tried to breathe again, but now that I knew we were all safe—even our unborn baby—I slipped back into that place. Back into the pain and the fear. I clung to Finn, my lungs filling up but not releasing the air. I watched as he tried to calm me, seeing his mouth move and hearing his voice, but I didn't hear a word he said.

The doctors rushed in, and Finn jumped back, covering his mouth as he watched me with tears in his eyes. He looked so scared. So broken. If I could talk, I'd tell him not to worry. If I could talk, I'd tell him everything was going to be okay.

But instead I was going to die.

Finn

A little while after Carrie woke up—and had a panic attack and gotten drugged until she passed out again—I rested my head back against the pleather chair, rubbing my throbbing temples, and yawned. I'd spent the last twenty minutes trying to do my best to explain to Carrie's parents why she'd had to be sedated when she'd woken up, and I was fucking beat.

I kept telling them that she'd be okay, that everything would be okay. But the truth was? I really had no fucking clue if that was true. None at all.

Carrie was barely hanging on to life, and she was terrified. I'd seen it in her eyes. I'd recognized that fear down to my soul. I knew it. I *was* it.

"But will she need to be sedated every time she wakes up?" Hugh asked, pacing back and forth. "Will she be okay?"

"Yes. She has to be." I closed my eyes. "Right now, all she remembers is the fear of dying. The pain. The shot that was fired...."

"Finn." Her mother walked up to me and hugged me. "Is she going to have...will she...?"

"Yeah. She might." I swallowed hard. "She might suffer from PTSD, like me."

What a pair we'd make.

The door opened, and someone knocked as it swung inward. The doctor stepped in, a tablet in his hand. "Mr. Coram?"

"Yes." I leapt to my feet, my heart racing. "I'm here."

"Sorry about the rush earlier, but—" He cut off, glancing at the Wallingtons. "Oh, you have company."

"It's her parents. They're fine."

"Wait. Are you...?" He broke off and bowed. "Senator Wallington.

Mrs. Wallington. It's an honor. I didn't realize—"

"Yes, he's a big deal. I get it." I stepped in front of them, blocking off the doctor's fangirling before it got too insane. "That's why there is security out there."

"Yeah, sorry about that. It's become necessary ever since news of the shooting hit all the major media outlets." Hugh extended a hand. "But, anyway, it's nice to meet you."

Mrs. Wallington smiled, ever the potential first lady. "Yes, it is."

"*Please.*" I waved an impatient hand. "What's going on, doctor? How is she doing?"

The doctor finally ripped his eyes off of the couple. "I think she'll be okay, with time. She needs to heal, and she needs to rest. I think, for now, sedating her is the best way to allow that to happen. If she keeps waking up and panicking like that, she could make her injuries worse."

Her mother wrung her hands. "But why is she panicking? Is she okay?"

"The mind is a tricky thing. She's just too traumatized to handle the reality of what happened to her right now. She might never be ready to handle all of that, which is why we'll have to keep a close eye on her." He gripped the tablet tight. "She was within seconds of bleeding out when she got here. Within seconds of dying. That takes a toll on a body."

"Jesus," I said, sinking into the chair.

"We can take care of her, Finn." Margie rested her hand on my shoulder. "You don't have to do this, considering...well, everything."

I stiffened. "I'm not leaving her."

"Not to pry, but are you military?"

I glanced away. "I was, yes."

"Ever go overseas?"

"Yeah." The voices in my head got louder, shouting for attention, but I shut them down. I didn't have time for them now. "And yes, I got injured over there. Saw things. Did things. Suffered from all of it."

"And you overcame it. Excellent. You'll understand why she is the way she is." The doctor nodded once. "You'll be a good support system."

I swallowed the panic trying to rise in my chest. How was I supposed to be a support system for her when I could barely keep my own shit together? "Yes."

The doctor must have noticed my hesitation. He narrowed his eyes on me. "Is everything okay?" the doctor asked, glancing at my in-laws a little hesitantly. "If you're not able to be there for—"

"I'll be there."

Her father cleared his throat and tugged on his tie. "Actually, they're separate—"

I stiffened. We might be separated, but if she needed me, I would be there. No questions asked. "We're fine," I said, my voice hard. "She has me, and I will take care of her. No matter what."

"We know, dear," said my mother-in-law, Margie, patting my hand. "But you can't do this alone. You have Susan to think about, too."

I closed my eyes. "I know. I am. I always am."

"You can all pitch in together," the doctor said, his tone soft. "As long as she has support, she'll heal. She'll recover. But if you've been experiencing difficulties, it's very important that she not be stressed—"

Understatement of the year. "We're fine," I said quickly, glowering at my in-laws. "I'm not leaving her side."

"If you've been fighting," the doctor repeated, locking gazes with me, "set it aside and make her your number-one priority. It's important she be kept as calm as possible so her wounds can heal."

I took a shaky breath and nodded. "Okay."

"What can we do?" her dad asked, holding hands with her mom. "How can we help her?"

"I'd say take care of their child, and come by to visit once or twice a day, but don't overdo it. Don't push her too hard." The doctor smiled at them. "She needs you, too, but I want her to focus on getting better so she can go home with her husband. It's the best thing for her."

"Right." Margie nodded. "That makes sense. She needs to feel safe with him."

"Exactly. She needs one strong connection, and in this case? It should be with him." The doctor headed for the door, but paused. "Unless there's a reason he shouldn't be her person? I'm sensing tension in the room. If it's better, she could stay with—"

"We're *fine*," I said.

"He's fine," Senator Wallington said at the same time.

"All right." The doctor stared at us and nodded once. "Again, it's an honor to meet you, sir. You'll have my vote."

"Thank you."

The doctor turned to me. "Mr. Coram? A word, please?"

"Yes." I looked at my in-laws. "I'll be right back."

"Take your time," Margie said, smiling tightly at me. "We'll stay with her."

Once we were out in the hallway, the doctor sighed. "I'm sorry to say it, but I have more bad news."

"What?" I fisted my hands. "What is it?"

He gripped my shoulder and squeezed reassuringly. "Regrettably, when the body goes into shock, it's often too much for a growing baby to handle. The body rebels, and it just kind of shuts down."

I narrowed my eyes, trying to figure out why the hell he was babbling on about babies and shock. Had he gotten his charts messed up? We weren't pregnant. "Okay?"

"What I'm saying is…" He hesitated. "The baby didn't make it."

"The baby…" I broke off, comprehension hitting me.

The throwing up. The weird behavior with the coffee. The way she'd jumped when I touched her nipples. And when she'd woken up, she'd asked if Susan was okay, and then she'd asked again, only this time she'd said "baby." I'd assumed she was confused and asking about Susan again. She hadn't been. She'd been pregnant.

And I'd missed all the signs.

"Mr. Coram?" the doctor said, alarm in his voice.

"Oh my God." I shook my head. Carrie had been pregnant, hadn't told me, and I'd told her the baby was okay. She'd think the baby was okay. "No."

"I know this is bad news," the doctor said, putting his hand on my arm. "But we were able to do a D&C while she was in surgery, so the good news is that the worst is over. She won't even really bleed much at all. Now the healing can start."

The healing. I hadn't even known I was going to be a father again, and now I was supposed to heal? "How did you know so soon? I mean, she hadn't even been late yet or anything."

He blinked. "She was two and a half months in. You knew, right?"

Two. Fucking. Months.

She'd had all that time to tell me we were having another baby, and she hadn't said a word. That's how little she trusted me right now. She probably hadn't told me because she'd thought it would make me upset. She'd thought it would make me worse.

My stomach hollowed out. I was going to fucking hurl.

"Shit. Shit. Shit."

I'd made her believe I wouldn't be happy about another baby. Another baby that we'd made. That's how far gone I'd been, yet I'd refused to accept that I needed help. Refused to admit it. She'd been scared to tell me. *Scared.*

I needed to get help. I needed to get better.

She needed me.

I'd been refusing to admit I needed help because I thought it made me weak. But it didn't. Carrie was right. I did need someone besides her. Dr. Montgomery had helped me see that, all those years ago.

Admitting I needed help made me stronger. It showed I was aware of my flaws, and that I'd do anything to keep my family safe. To keep my family whole.

I needed help, and I'd get it.

For her. For Susan. And for *me*.

"Are you okay?" the doctor asked. His voice sounded miles away. "Mr. Coram?"

I thought of Carrie, and how scared she was, and how much she needed me right now. It pulled me back into the light. "Yeah. Sorry." I dragged my hands down my face. "Thank you for telling me."

Once the doctor left, I took a second to compose myself, and walked back into her room in a trance. Hugh sat in the chair, his face hidden behind his hands. With the news of the lost baby, I'd forgotten they were here.

My gaze fell on Carrie. She looked so pale. So lifeless. It scared the shit out of me. I walked over to her side and sat down on the side of the bed. She'd been so worried about me this past week and a half. So scared for me.

And I'd been too blind to see it.

To listen to her. Never again.

I kissed her forehead and closed my eyes. "I'm here. And I'll be here when you wake up. I'm not going anywhere ever again."

Hugh watched me. "Are you saying what I think you're saying?"

"I'm saying if she can forgive me for being blind," I took a deep breath, "then I'm not going anywhere. And I'm going back to Dr. Montgomery. It's time."

"Good." Margie laid her hand on my shoulder. "She's been so worried about you."

I swallowed past the aching lump in my throat. "I know." I closed my eyes and opened them again, finding a new strength I hadn't realized I had within me. "But no more. Never again. It's time for me to take care of her, not the other way around."

Carrie moaned, and Hugh rushed to her side, grabbing her hand. "It's okay, Princess. We're here."

She quieted.

I swallowed hard.

"I can't keep watching her in pain like this," Hugh whispered, his eyes locked on Carrie's pale face. He was obviously on the verge of a panic attack. I'd had enough panic to last me a fucking lifetime. "She's never going to—"

"You will, and you'll do it with a smile on your face," I said, my voice harder than ever before with him. Even harder than when he'd told me I wasn't good enough for her, all those years ago. "Because you owe it to her. You owe her this."

He paled, but nodded. "I know. It's my fault. This is all my fault."

"That's not what I meant," I said, feeling like shit for making the man feel worse. My head wasn't on straight right now, but I knew one thing—she didn't need us sobbing and whimpering over her right now. "It's not your fault."

Her father insisted it was his fault, since the man had been intent on punishing him through Carrie. The fucker who had tried to kill my Carrie. I'd killed him, and I didn't even feel bad about it. Not really. If anything, I wish I could do it again.

He'd almost taken Carrie's life, and he deserved to rot in hell. I hoped he was. I hoped heaven and hell were real, and he was burning with Satan's spike up his fucking ass for all eternity. And if that damned me to hell as well, then so be it. I'd spend my own eternity fucking him up even more.

He'd killed my baby.

"It is." Hugh covered his face. "It's my fault."

"I know you feel like this is all on you, but it's not." I hugged the man close. We'd had our issues once, but he'd been good to me for years. I could never be anything less to him. "You didn't know he'd escaped. You had no way of knowing."

He deflated, almost as if I'd removed a huge weight from his shoulders. "Thank you." He hugged me back, his grip tight and loving. "Thank you, son."

I blinked back the stinging warning of impending tears, the ones I'd been holding off for what felt like years, gave him a man pat on the back, and stepped back. "There's nothing to thank me for. It's the truth."

Margie locked eyes with me, nodding once and mouthing, "Thank you."

I glanced away uneasily.

A moan came from the bed behind me. I rushed to her side just in time to see her bright blue eyes. I soaked them in, knowing it wouldn't last long. She was high as a kite and sedated. She'd be out cold in another minute or two. "Hey, Ginger."

She glanced up at me, her bright blue eyes glazed over from the morphine. "Why do you keep calling me that?" she asked. "That's not my name."

Yep. She was high as a kite. We'd had almost this exact conversation all those years ago when we'd met. I forced a smile and tugged on her red hair gently. "Because it suits you. Why? Don't you like it?"

"I don't think so." She bit her lower lip. "It annoys me, but it also makes me…"

"Want to hit me?" I supplied, hoping to help. "You told me that once. It's a feeling I bring out in you fairly often."

"No." She glanced up at me, and looked away quickly. Her cheeks pinked. "It makes me feel…" She smiled dreamily, her eyes watered over.

She didn't finish, so I quirked a brow. "Yeah?"

I was trying not to laugh, but she was acting so different it was hard not to. I'd never seen her like this. She didn't even drink wine because of me.

That must be why the drugs had hit her so hard.

She nodded. "Yep. That's it."

"What's it?" I asked, chuckling. "You have to say it out loud, Ginger."

"Oh. I thought I did." She looked up at me. "I think it makes me happy. And it makes me think you love me. It makes me think of laughing, and teasing, and...*kissing*." she whispered. "Lots of kissing."

My heart stuttered, and then sped up quickly. Leaning down, I stopped when our noses were practically touching and our gazes were locked. Lowering my voice so her parents didn't hear, I said, "That's because we do that a lot, too. Among other things."

Her cheeks went even pinker.

Jesus, it was adorable. She hadn't blushed for me in years. She was a hell of a lot like the Carrie I'd met in college, in more ways than one. She bit her lip in the way she always did when she wanted to flirt with me.

"I bet we do." She giggled. Carrie never giggled. "I kinda want to kiss you now."

Something else inside of me gave way. Something I couldn't listen to right now. "Maybe later." I squeezed her hand and straightened. "Your parents are here right now, and they want to say hello before they leave."

"Oh." She peeked over my shoulder, her grip on me not relaxing even the slightest. I looked at them, giving them a reassuring smile. I tried to see what she saw. Her father's gray hair was messy for the first time ever, and her mother was in a tizzy. They didn't look like the possible first lady and president. They looked like worried parents. "Hi, Mom. Hi, Dad. I think I'm drunk."

They went on the other side of the bed. "Hello, Princess," Hugh said, bending down and kissing the bandages on the left side of Carrie's head. "I'm very, very glad to see those blue eyes again. Glad you're okay."

She glanced at me and gave a small smile to her father. "I'm glad too. Dying would have sucked. I think."

I choked on a half-laugh, half-sob, and Carrie grinned.

"Yes, it would have," her mother said, leaning in and kissing her. "We would have missed you."

"I'd hope so," I said drily.

Carrie smiled wider. "I'm sorry to put you both through the scare. I hear it was quite...messy."

"Very." Hugh looked at me, scanning my clothes. I knew he was remembering how much blood I'd had on me when he'd found us in the foyer. He'd never see those clothes again because I'd thrown them out. I hadn't wanted Carrie to see how much I'd looked like an extra out of some fucking horror film. "But you're okay now, so that's all that matters."

Carrie glanced at her lap, at our joined hands, then at me. "I think I'm in good hands here."

"You are." I squeezed her fingers. "I'll be here with you the whole time."

"We will be, too," Margie said.

"Well, not *here* here. We can't all sleep in this small room," Hugh said, smiling. It wobbled, but he held it together pretty damn good. "We'll be at your house, taking care of S—"

"Things," I said quickly. "The plants and whatnot."

I didn't want her to go back into another panic attack. She needed rest, and hearing Susan's name might remind her of the baby she hadn't told me about. And if I had to tell her about the baby, she might break down again.

She needed to heal a little more first.

Hugh flushed. "Right."

"Th-Thank you," Carrie said, looking confused. She yawned, and her eyes drifted shut. "I...I'm sorry. I don't...I'm..."

And then she fell asleep. Just like that.

"Carrie?" I waved my hand in front of her face, and she didn't move. *This* was not like my Carrie. My Carrie tossed and turned for hours before finally settling into sleep. The drugs must have done her in. "I think maybe she's tired," I said drily.

Margie laughed and covered her mouth right away. Her eyes filled up with tears, and she backed away. "W-We'll go. Let her rest. Please, if anything changes, let us know."

"Call us no matter what," Hugh said, catching my stare. "Please. Take good care of our baby."

"I will," I promised. "And you take good care of mine."

"We will." They hugged me, and I tried to hug them back, but when I tugged on my hand, Carrie didn't let go. And I'd be damned before I made her. "We'll relieve Marie from her babysitting duties now."

Marie was Carrie's best friend. I'd been fielding calls from her all night long.

"Thank you."

After they walked out, I stared at the chair across the room. My injured leg hurt like a bitch, but I wouldn't be able to reach it from here. I stood there for I don't know how long, my leg throbbing and my eyes getting heavier by the moment.

At some point, hours later, I crawled into the bed, keeping clear of any tubes or injuries on Carrie, wrapped my arm over her, and passed the hell out.

Having Carrie back in my arms gave me the first real sleep I'd had since…

I didn't even know.

chapter
sixteen

Carrie

I backed up slowly, my heart hammering in my ears as I held both hands out, trying to seem as unthreatening as possible. "Please. Don't do this."

The man laughed and held the gun out at me. "I'm going to kill you, and your baby, and the man you say you love—but who doesn't love you anymore. If he did, he'd be here."

"No. That's not true."

"He doesn't love you. No one does." He grinned evilly. "And now you're going to die alone."

"Please! Don't—" The gunshot boomed, and I gasped, clutching my chest and fighting the arms that held me down. "No! Let me go!"

"*Carrie*," a voice said, his voice hurried and scared. "Wake up. I'm here. Please, open those eyes. Wake up. You're safe. I have you."

I fought the hands holding me down. Something clogged my nose, so I pulled at that. Maybe they were trying to suffocate me since the bullet hadn't done me in. I had to escape. Had to live. Had to...

I yanked the tubes out of my nose. "*Finn.*"

"I'm here. I'm right here." Hands shook me. "Please, wake up. They're going to have to sedate you again if you don't stop this."

That voice. I *knew* that voice.

Slowly, I opened my eyes. The lights were way too bright and they hurt, but I blinked the tears away. I stopped fighting. "F-Finn?" He had an aura around his head from the light that looked like a halo. He looked like an angel. I choked on a sob. "Oh my God. I'm dead. I'm dead, aren't I?"

"No. You're here, and so am I. Feel me." He held my hand to his cheek. He was warm to the touch, and he had a lot of scruff that scratched my hand. "See? Not a ghost."

Tears escaped my eyes, and I forced a calm breath. "It's you. You came."

"Did you ever doubt I would?" He smiled at me, but it didn't reach his eyes. His eyes were sad. So, so sad. "Can you let them get you resituated? Will you stop fighting them?"

"O-Of course." I glanced at the nurses that surrounded my bed. They all looked as if they'd been in a tornado. "I'm sorry."

"Nothing to be sorry for." Finn nodded at them, then turned back to me with a tender smile. He brushed my hair out of my eyes with his hand, his touch soft and sweet. "But I'm sorry this happened to you, Ginger."

"It's okay. It's not…" I broke off, horror coming through my veins. I pressed a hand to my stomach, somehow knowing it was no longer carrying anything. I felt so empty. "The baby."

His smile faded, and his eyes filled with tears. "Carrie…"

"*No*." My heartbeat accelerated, and I slapped a nurse's hands away when she reached for me. "No. Please, no."

"I'm so sorry, Carrie. But the baby…it didn't…there was too much shock to your body." Finn tried to hug me close, but I pushed him off. "Carrie, *please*."

I shook my head, a sob escaping me. It hurt to cry, but I couldn't stop it. "Not our baby. I didn't even get to tell you yet. You didn't…*no*."

The nurse reached for me again, and suddenly I was back in that place. Back in my foyer, with a gun pointed at me. I bucked my back, fighting for my life. Fighting for my child's life. Everyone tried to hold me down, but I didn't let them. It was over. I'd lost my baby, and I had nothing left to hold on to.

Finn called my name, and I heard him, but I didn't look at him. I just fought until it all went black, and I couldn't fight anymore.

I was screaming, running for my life. The footsteps came even closer, faster, louder. They echoed against the walls, taunting me. I knew he was going to catch me. I wasn't fast enough. Wasn't smart enough. He would get me, and he'd kill me. He was going to kill me. I screamed again, the sound piercing and loud.

I was going to die, here in this pitch-black hallway if I didn't...if I didn't...*wake up*. With a lurching breath, I wrenched my eyes open. Instead of a madman trying to kill me, I saw a bunch of IV tubes and the square tiles of the hospital ceiling. The room was deathly quiet, aside from the beeping of my machines, even though I'd been so sure I'd been screaming louder than a banshee.

I was in bed, and I was safe.

I gasped for air, struggling to ground myself. Obviously, I hadn't actually been running for my life. Instead, I'd been having a nightmare where some faceless man was chasing me, a gun in his hand. I tried to lift my arm to wipe away the sweat off my forehead, but someone held on to it tightly.

Turning my head slowly, I came face to face with the most handsome man I'd ever seen. His eyes were closed, and half of his face was buried beside my pillow, but I recognized him instantly. Despite the confusion and the pain and the fear, I knew him.

He was my husband. *Finn*.

Then I remembered. I'd been shot, and I was in the hospital. I had a feeling I had been for a while, but for some reason I couldn't remember how long. The world spun a bit, and I turned my head, squinting at the square receptacle that held all my meds. Scanning the names, I realized why I didn't remember anything.

They'd been sedating me. And I was still on morphine.

Why had they sedated me?

Biting down on my lip, I looked back at Finn. Slowly, I reached out and touched his cheek gently. As soon as I touched him, I felt calmer. As if he would keep me safe from the nightmares. But what if this was the nightmare? What if he woke up and shot me in the face? The drugs I was on were doing weird things to my head. I'd even had a dream that Susan had tried to kill me with a rope.

The terror never shut off in my dreams.

Finn mumbled in his sleep, rubbed his face against my palm, and let out a small snore. His full lips pursed before relaxing again. I smiled, because it was so human. So real. And that's when I knew I was awake. Alive. Safe.

He stirred, rubbing his nose. I traced the scar that ran across his forehead, down toward his eye, and sadness intermingled with memories. This is what had started us down the path we'd taken. We'd fought our way to find our love again, back then, and we could do it again. We'd come through it eventually. We *had* to.

I tried to sit up, twisting my shoulder the wrong way. I was highly medicated, but I still felt *that*. I gasped from the startling pain.

"What's wrong?" Finn's asked before his lids even flew open. He was awake within seconds, breathing heavily. "Carrie?"

"Hi," I whispered.

He reached out to touch me, but he pulled back before actually doing so. "Is this another dream?"

Funny. I'd wondered the same thing. Guess now I knew what it felt like to be unaware of what was real and what wasn't. "No. It's me." Knowing what had helped me believe it was real, I caught his hand and held it to my cheek. "See? It's real."

"You're awake." His eyes filled with wonder. "They said you wouldn't wake up from the drugs till tonight. You're early."

My lips curved into a smile. "Want me to fall back asleep?"

"No." He grinned back at me. "Never."

"I'm…I'm glad you're here." I glanced up at him. "I wasn't sure if you would be."

"There's nowhere else I'd rather be than here. Now." His gaze skimmed down my body. "Though I'd rather it wasn't under these circumstances. How are you feeling? You gasped when you woke up."

"I'm fine. I was having a nightmare before I woke up, and I jerked awake. It hurt." I swallowed hard. "A man was chasing me and trying to kill me. It felt so real. But then I woke up and saw you, and I knew it was just a dream."

He visibly relaxed. "Yeah, you're going to get those types of dreams for a while. They'll feel real. So real you can taste the sweat rolling off your forehead, and smell the fear in the air."

"Those are the dreams you have?"

He locked his gaze on me. "They are."

My heart wrenched. I finally understood what he felt, but it might be too late. I might be too late. I licked my parched lips. "How long have I been asleep?"

Hesitating, he glanced away before answering. "They had to sedate you." He tugged on his hair. "It's been a little under a week."

"A *week*?" I struggled to sit up, but failed. I just didn't have the strength yet. "Why? What happened? What's wrong with me?"

"Shh." He caught my hand and ran his thumb over the backs of my knuckles. "You were fighting the nurses. Ripping off the oxygen mask and refusing to let them help you."

And I remembered now. I remembered waking up, and Finn being there. Countless times, I'd woken up and found him at my bed. He'd always been there. He'd always tried to calm me, but I'd kept fighting being awake. Kept fighting real life. Because I'd lost our baby. The baby

I hadn't even had a chance to tell him about.

He'd had to find out after I'd already lost him.

"No." I shook my head slowly. "God, no."

Finn crumbled. "Please don't do it again."

"We lost our baby." I cradled my empty stomach. "It's gone. He took it. It's gone. Our baby is gone."

"I'm so sorry," Finn whispered, his voice as broken as his eyes. "I wish I could take it back. Wish we could go back. I want to go back."

"We can't. It's gone," I whispered, tears rolling down my face. "It's all gone."

He hugged me close, kissing my forehead and trembling. "I'm sorry. I wanted to save you. I should have saved you. I wanted to. I'm so sorry."

Something in his voice snapped me out of my own pain. Then I realized what it was. It was his pain. I could feel it. Watching me like this was sending him even darker into his own abyss. I was dragging him down with me. This might be ripping me apart, but it was doing the same to him.

He was terrified I'd slip back into my panic. Terrified I blamed him. I could tell. I forced myself to focus on him. "Our baby, Finn. He killed our baby."

"I know. I'm sorry. I have to do this. I'm sorry." When he saw me watching him, he froze. He'd been about to press the nurses' button. "Carrie?"

"I'm here," I whispered. "It hurts. It hurts so much."

He nodded, not speaking. He didn't need to. I could feel his pain, and he could feel mine. Instead of meaningless words, he did what I needed most. He pulled me close and held me. He smoothed my hair back from my head and kissed me, telling me over and over again how much he loved me.

And he didn't let go.

Sometime later, my tears had dried, but I couldn't stop the pain. I stared up at the ceiling, clinging to Finn for dear life. I could feel his eyes on me, but I didn't dare look at him. It might break me all over again.

"I'm sorry, Carrie," he whispered, hugging me closer. "So fucking sorry. I hope you know that. Hope you believe me someday."

As if snapping out of a trance, I jumped. Slowly, I turned to him. He was ashen, and he looked a step away from death's door. "Are you okay?" I asked.

He glanced at me in surprise. As if he couldn't believe I'd talked to him again. Maybe he'd thought I had fallen back asleep. It made me wonder how many times he'd apologized over the past few days, talking to me while I slept.

Begging me to hear him.

"I'm fine." He forced a smile. "We need to worry about you, not me."

I stared at him. "But you're in pain."

"Only you would be in a hospital bed and be worried about me. I'm constantly amazed by you. By your heart." He kissed the tip of my nose. It did weird things to my pulse. "You're always worrying about me, and it constantly staggers me that you could care so much after all we've been through. I've never deserved you, and I never really will, but I never want to let you go. I'm selfish like that."

"I don't think that's selfish at all." I reached out and cupped his cheek, resting my thumb on the bottom of his chin. He had a tiny dimple there. "I think it's just right."

I rested his hand over my heart, which leapt at his touch.

"Carrie..." His eyes got a little glazed, and he looked away. After he cleared this throat, he turned back to me with a smile. "You need to rest some more. You have to get better." He kissed my temple. "So I'm going to tell you a bedtime story."

I didn't say anything. I was too tired to talk. He rested his head against the back of my bed, and I cuddled up next to him as best as I could with all the pain, tubes, and wires coming out of me. He took a deep breath, and I closed my eyes. The sound of his steady heartbeat was already lulling me to sleep.

"Once upon a time, there was a beautiful red-haired girl on the beach. She was a princess. A beautiful, kind princess. She'd just escaped from a fancy ball because she didn't like parties. When she escaped, standing in the shadows was a man. An ordinary man, no match for her beauty and grace. From the shadows of the beach, the man watched her. He couldn't look away. The girl was so pretty and alluring. All he wanted to do was know her."

I smiled sleepily. "This story sounds familiar."

"Shh. Close your eyes and relax." His arm tightened around me. "But the man couldn't talk to her. He was supposed to be her bodyguard. He worked for her father, the king of the village." He leaned in and kissed my bandage. "And he wasn't supposed to like her like he did. When they..."

I didn't hear the rest.

I fell asleep, cradled in the arms of the man I loved.

chapter

seventeen

Finn

Six days later, almost three full weeks after the shooting, I sat in my truck, glowering at the vans parked outside of our house. Ever since word had gotten out that there had been an attempt on Senator Wallington's daughter's life, the media had been relentless in their desire to know all the gory details. Everyone wanted to hear about it.

They followed me everywhere. They'd been there when I left for the police station to give my statement for the ten millionth time, and they'd been there when I'd gotten out hours later. And then they'd followed me home.

At least Carrie was safely tucked away inside. She'd been home for a day and a half, and we'd somehow managed to sneak her out the back door of the hospital when we'd left. At least she'd been able to avoid the frenzy that was now our life.

I took a deep breath and opened the door. Immediately, reporters started acting like seagulls fighting over the same fucking fish.

"How's your wife?"

"What did the police say?'

"How's it feel to live in the same house your wife was shot in?"

The questions never stopped coming. I ignored them all. The

security guards kept them off my property, but that didn't stop them from shouting questions at me. I couldn't wait for a celebrity to be caught sharing naked photos or making a porno.

Then they'd move on to the next hot thing.

Head down, I made my way to the door. Hugh and Margie were inside, watching over Carrie while I went to work. As much as I wished I could stay home all week long taking care of her, it wasn't possible. I'd been out of work for too long, and now Carrie was, too. We were financially stable, but that didn't mean we could take months off of work and not feel the strain.

On top of that, I'd had another stop on the way home from work, before the police station. I'd had to see Dr. Montgomery. I'd started going again, and she was a huge help. After Carrie had been injured, I'd known it was a necessary step. Now, more so than ever, I needed to be strong.

Carrie needed me.

I unlocked the door, my eyes on the red stained concrete. The blood had come out, but the stain wouldn't. It was a constant reminder that I hadn't been here when I should have been. That wouldn't happen again. I wouldn't let it.

Closing the door behind me, I listened for my family. Carrie's soft voice filled my senses, and I closed my eyes, leaning against the door. I let her soft musical voice wash over me, taking away all the voices that tried to distract me. Taking away the darkness that threatened to overcome me.

She was my light. My flame. My love.

"Is that you, Finn?" Hugh asked, coming into the foyer. He wore a suit and his hair was as impeccable as ever. "It is. How did it go?"

I tugged on my tie, loosening it. "Good. Work was crazy, the police station was swarmed with reporters." I averted my eyes. "But they didn't make it to the therapist. At least they don't know about that yet."

"Don't look away like that, son." Hugh walked over to me and rested his hand on my shoulder. "There's nothing to be ashamed of. Nothing at all. I know you've been having a tough time, even before she was injured, and this can only be making it harder. Hell, I'm having nightmares, too."

I blinked. "You are?"

"Yes." He tugged on his collar. "But what I'm saying is I know why you were suffering, and I still say there's nothing to be ashamed of. Your father would be proud of you. Proud of the man you've become."

I swallowed hard, finding it hard to breathe. This man, though once my enemy, was now so much more. My father had been gone for so long, and Hugh had filled that void. For so long, he'd been there. And I was ashamed to admit it, but I'd taken that for granted. "Sir...I...thank you."

"I love you, son." He crossed the room and hugged me tight. So tight that he might have cracked a rib, but it felt fucking amazing. "We all do."

I hugged him back, blinking away the moisture in my eyes. "I love you, too."

Margie came in, an emotional smile on her face. Her eyes were wetter than mine. "I agree. Your father would be so proud of you. We all are."

I let go of Hugh, and he stepped back. We both straightened our jackets. "Thank you, Margie."

"Dinner is in the stove." She picked up her jacket, and Hugh rushed to her side to help her get it on. "It's lasagna. I know it's not as good as yours, but I figured any home-cooked meal would make your first day back at work easier."

I hugged her. "It does. Thank you."

"Thank you." She patted my cheek. "She's waiting for you. She's in good spirits today."

"That's good." I nodded and swallowed hard. Carrie might seem as if she was in good spirits, but I knew better. It was an act to make us all feel better. She was still taking care of us, even though we were supposed to be the ones taking care of her. "I'll head in after I reset the lock code."

I watched them go, setting the code back to alarm after they left. Through the window, I watched them stop to talk to the media. Senator Wallington gestured to the house, then to himself. He was probably asking them to respect our privacy.

He might as well have saved his breath.

After they got in their limo, I let the curtain fall back into place. Straightening my spine, I headed for the living room with a bright smile on my face. She wasn't the only one who was putting on an act. I was too. As much as she felt she needed to be strong for me...

I felt it a million times worse, because I hadn't been there for her. I should have been there for her.

"Honey, I'm home," I called out, my voice as light as I could possibly manage. "You should have seen my desk. It was piled to the ceiling with assignments, I swear."

"Lots of computer codes needing to be written and systems to be tested?" she asked, turning to me with a smile. Susan sat on her lap, playing with the beaded necklace Carrie wore. I'd bought it for her three years ago for her birthday. "Did you save the world, one code at a time?"

"You know it." I sat beside them and kissed Carrie's temple. When Susan saw me, she dropped the necklace and beamed at me. "Now I'm home with both of my princesses."

"Dah!" Susan wailed, her fists flying. She reached out for me. "Dah!"

"Come here." I caught her under her armpits and lifted her high, making a silly face at her. She giggled and patted my face—which was more of a slap. "Ow."

Susan pulled on my lower lip, and I made a gurgling sound. She giggled even more. Carrie leaned back and smiled, but her eyes were filled with sadness. It broke my heart to see her like this. Trying to act as if she was strong and didn't feel pain.

But I'd learned something lately. Pain was something you couldn't ignore. It needed to be felt, and it wouldn't shut up until you acknowledged its existence. It wouldn't just go away. Pain was a stubborn asshole like that. Kinda like me.

"Finn." She readjusted herself on the couch, meeting my eyes. She still looked so pale and weak. And yet, somehow, she seemed stronger, too. As if she'd come to some sort of decision, and I was scared to know what it might be. "We need to talk."

Those words never failed to fill me with dread. The smile on my face slid away, and I swallowed. "Okay. Can it wait until she's down for the night?"

"I'd rather do it now." She tucked her hair behind her ear, glancing at me nervously. She was moving so much better now, as if she was actually healed. I knew better. "I don't want to lose my nerve."

Susan whacked me in the eye. I flinched. "She's got a better arm than her mother. Geez."

"Finn."

I winced again. This time because of her, though. Not Susan. "I know."

"When I got hurt, you weren't living here. You'd...left." She lifted a knee and hugged it close, resting her chin on it. "Then I got hurt, and you swooped in to take care of me. Thank you for that, by the way. After everything we'd been through, you still...you still..."

"Because of everything we'd been through, I had to." I turned away from her, knowing what was coming and scared as hell. Susan watched me, her expression way too somber. It was as if she knew what was happening, too, and didn't like it. Neither did I. "Did you expect me not to take care of you? You're my wife, Carrie."

"I know." She closed her eyes for a second before she opened them. She looked so sad. So alone. "But I'm better now. I don't need to be taken care of anymore."

"You don't have to finish. I know what you're going to say. You want me to leave," I said, my voice hollow. I couldn't help it. My heart was getting ripped out of my chest all over again. "You want me to get out again."

She glanced at me, tears in her eyes. "That's not it."

"Then what is it?" Susan squirmed and wiggled toward the floor, so I put her down. I immediately missed her warmth. Her smile. Everything. "What do you want?"

"I want you to be happy." She swiped a tear away with her hand. "It's all I've ever wanted for you."

"It's all I ever wanted for you, too," I said.

"You left me," she said, hugging her leg even tighter. "You walked away."

"I know," I whispered. My eyes stung, but I refused to give in. "I shouldn't have done that. It's my fault you're hurt. It's my fault you lost our baby."

She whipped her head toward me. "Don't. Don't go there."

"How could I not?" I stood up and tugged on my hair. Susan played with my pants leg, jerking on it hard. "If I hadn't walked away, I would have been here. If I hadn't walked away, you wouldn't have thought it was me knocking on that door. If I hadn't been in denial about needing help, I wouldn't have run."

She shook her head, tears streaming down her face. "This isn't your fault. None of it is."

"That's what Dr. Montgomery says, too." I covered my face and closed my eyes. Closed out the world. "But I don't believe her, and I don't believe you, either."

"You went to see her again?"

"I did." I let out a harsh laugh and dropped my hands. "But it's too late."

Susan still sat at my feet, watching me with a wrinkled brow. I tried to force a smile for her, and it must have worked despite the fact that I felt like I was dying. She smiled up at me and then crawled away. I felt like an empty shell of a man right now. Carrie was kicking me out, and this time it would be for good.

My epiphany about getting help had come too late.

"Finn."

I looked at Carrie again, memorizing everything about her. The way her soft red hair framed her face. The way the later afternoon sunlight streamed through the curtains, making her blue eyes seem even bluer. The soft yellow hues that made her seem more fragile than ever, and the tears streaming down her face. I didn't want to forget a single detail because this was our last time together.

This was the end.

"I know." I curled my hands into fists to stop myself from grabbing her and begging her to let me stay. "I'll go."

I walked toward the door, but she reached out and grabbed my elbow. "Wait."

"Why? If you want me to go, it's best if I just…go. I love you with everything I have, and I want to stay. I want you to want me to stay. I want to be here, at your side, until we're old and wrinkled and eating chocolate pudding with our dentures out."

She covered her mouth, tears falling out faster than before. Then she lowered her hand and shook her head, struggling to speak. "I-I want that, too."

"I know you did. We both did. But you've changed your mind, and I don't blame you at all. It's my fault that this is happening. I walked away, after swearing to never do it again. I broke your heart, even though I swore I wouldn't." I slammed my fist on my thigh. It hurt. I welcomed the pain. "I broke every single promise I ever made to you. I ruined everything."

"Don't say that." She licked her lips, her eyes locked on mine. "It's not true. You didn't do any of this on purpose. You didn't choose to be injured on assignment. You didn't choose to suffer from PTSD. You didn't choose to get in a car accident. And you certainly didn't choose to hurt me again. Not really."

My heart sped up, even though I knew I was being foolish to hope she'd changed her mind. "But I did. I hurt you."

She hesitated, but nodded once. "You did."

"That's why I have to go. I love you so damn much, but I know you're better off without me. I'd never be the one to say it, but you're saying it." I stared at Susan. She stacked some blocks on top of each other. She had her tongue out, caught between her lips, and she looked so much like Carrie did when she was concentrating that it hurt. "You're asking me to leave, and you're right. It's for the best."

"Wait," she said again, struggling to her feet.

"Damn it, I can't," I said, closing my eyes. I couldn't look at her right now. She was so pretty and so not mine. Not anymore. "If I wait, I'll try to talk you out of it. I'll selfishly beg you to let me stay, when you're making the right choice. I'll selfishly remind you of all the good years we've had, and I'll try to make you forget the rest. I need to go, now, without looking at you again. Because I swear, Carrie, it gets harder to walk away every time. Every time I walk away, I die even more inside. I don't know if I'll be able to survive another time. If I'll have enough left of me to go on."

"But you see." She made a broken sound and cupped my face. I still didn't open my eyes. I couldn't. If I did, I'd break. "I don't *want* you to go."

My heart stuttered to a stop. I gripped her arms, still not looking at her. "What?"

"Look at me."

"Carrie…" I opened my eyes. She stared up at me, her blue eyes so deep and meaningful it stole the breath right out of my lungs. "Don't."

"Don't what? Don't ask you to stay? Don't ask you to leave?"

I shook my head. "I don't know."

"The reason I told you to go is simple. I thought you were only here because you had to be. To take care of me while I was weak." She let go of me and lowered her hand to her lap. It shook. "I'm not weak anymore. I'm stronger. I can lift Susan. I can cook food. I'll be fine."

My heart splintered and fell to the floor. "But you're not better. You might feel better, but I see the pain in your eyes. I feel it."

"I know." She stroked my jaw with her thumbs. "I feel yours, too. It hurts to see you so alone. So scared. So…so…"

I was hurting her. I wanted to stop. "I'll go."

"Don't."

"Carrie…"

"I don't want you to go. I swear it." She reached up on tiptoe and kissed me, her lips gentle and soft in a barely there caress. "I'd never want you to leave me, Finn. I'd never *want* that. I love you, and I want to spend the rest of my life with you, too. I want to have more babies and watch them grow up. I want to grow old with you, and I want that chocolate pudding, too. And the dentures." She let out a nervous laugh. "I want it all, with you. But know this—if you want to leave…if that's still what you want—"

"No. I don't." I cupped the back of her head, my hand shaking so hard it was a wonder I didn't pull her hair out. "I want to stay. I want to stay so damn bad."

"Then *stay*."

My splintered heart pieced itself back together, inch by painful inch. "Are you sure? After everything I've done…everything I've said."

She smiled up at me, tears in her eyes. "I'm positive as a proton."

"Da!" Susan pulled on my pants leg. "Da! Up!"

"I love you." I kissed Carrie, keeping it light. When I pulled back, I stared down into those blue eyes that had always mesmerized me. The ones I couldn't live without. I dropped my forehead on hers, breathing in her sweet scent. "I love you, I love you, I love you."

She shuddered and clung to me. "I love you, too."

And then I kissed her. A full-on, tongues entwining, passionate kiss that made so many promises, all over again. Promises I intended to keep this time.

"*Ma!*" Susan yelled, smacking Carrie's leg. "*Da!*"

Choking on a laugh, I broke off the kiss. "I think she wants in on this," I whispered, smiling against Carrie's lips. "To be continued?"

She nodded. "To be continued."

I bent down and picked Susan up, and she snuggled into my chest, yawning. I smiled at Carrie, who smiled back at me. For the first time in weeks, I let out a relieved breath. We'd fought for our love. Fought for each other.

And we'd won.

We'd really fucking won.

chapter eighteen

Finn

Later that night, I closed the door to Susan's room and took a deep breath. The evening had passed in a quiet fashion, feeling extremely normal and happy and unreal. We'd played with Susan and had a family night just like we used to before the night it had all changed. It had been a perfect evening.

Life was normal again, and I might be getting there, too.

When I pushed off the wall and headed for the stairs, I only made it two steps before I stopped in front of our bedroom. The lights were dimmed, and they'd been off when I'd come up. Had Carrie snuck upstairs when I'd been busy with Susan? I peeked my head inside... and froze. Just fucking froze.

She'd come upstairs, all right.

And gotten *naked*.

She stood in the middle of the room, wearing nothing but a pair of fuck-me heels and her long red hair that I loved. Her pale skin screamed for my touch, as did her hard nipples. Hell, it all did. But I stayed where I was, not daring to move so much as an inch.

Her newest scar, the evidence of my inability to protect her when she'd needed me most, stood out against her pale skin. I stared at it, swallowing past the pain the sight caused me. But I forced myself to look at the rest of her, taking it all in.

She was so gorgeous, in every way possible, and I was the luckiest man in the world. "Fuck," I said, my voice somehow reverent despite the word I uttered. "Carrie."

She cocked her head and played with a curl. "Yeah?"

She looked so fucking brave. So beautiful. As if she had no doubt of her welcome whatsoever. And why would she doubt it? She was always welcome.

But I hadn't expected *this*.

"You're—" My voice broke off into a moan when she dropped the curl and trailed her hand down her own hip. I rubbed my jaw. "Jesus."

Her lips curled into a satisfied smile. "Why are you still all the way over there?"

"Are you sure?" I collapsed against the wall, trying to keep my eyes strictly on her face. "Are you feeling okay? Physically? Emotionally? I don't want to make it worse. Don't want to hurt you. I don't know if you're ready..."

"Finn?" She sashayed—yes, fucking *sashayed*—over to me, her lips still curved upward. "There will never be a day where making love to you makes me feel worse."

She'd used my words back on me.

"I'm sure you feel ready," I said, licking my dry lips. "But if you're not sure—"

She stopped in front of me and grabbed the collar of my button-up shirt. "Do you want me or not?"

She pressed up against me, and I knew my answer was no longer necessary. She now knew with crystal clear clarity exactly how much I wanted her. I answered anyway. "Of course I do. I want you so much it hurts. I always have and always will."

She un-popped a button. "I can make the hurt better."

I groaned.

"Finn?" Another button, followed by another.

"Yeah?" I said through my clenched jaw.

"I get to be in charge first. That way you don't have to worry about being too rough or hurting me by accident."

I cocked a brow and tried to ignore the need she was bringing out in me with every soft touch of her fingers. I'd need all the control I could muster if she wanted to be in control. "Okay."

"Good." She undid the last button and opened my shirt. She stared at my chest and licked her lips. When she glanced up at me, her blue eyes were sparkling. "You don't have to call me sir, though."

She unbuttoned my pants.

"Carrie..." She unzipped my pants and slid them down my legs. I clenched my fists, forcing myself to remain still. "You're still healing. We have to take it slow."

"I'm fine."

She cupped my cock, squeezing it with the perfect amount of pressure. A groan escaped me, despite my best efforts to hold it back. "*Fuuuuck.*"

This would normally be the time that I would toss her onto the bed and fuck her until she came so many times I lost count. But I forced myself to stand still. To let her explore my body, since she'd asked for it.

"So many bad words coming out of your mouth," she teased. "Yet you're just standing there..."

"That's because you asked me to," I gritted. "Normally I'd be fucking you by now."

"Then I guess I'll have to fuck you instead." She dropped down to her knees, glancing up at me through long red lashes that would tempt the devil himself. "Won't I?"

I fisted my hands. "You have no idea what kind of fire you're playing with, Ginger."

"Oh, but I do." She yanked my boxers down and wrapped her fingers around my cock. Leaning in, she stopped before touching me with those sweet red lips of hers. "I really, *really* do."

She closed her mouth around me and swirled her tongue over the head of my cock. I dropped my head against the wall, my eyes rolling back in my head, and I curled my hands into her hair. "*Yes.* Fuck, yes."

She moaned and took more of me in, experimenting with my length and her own mouth. It felt so fucking good, and then it felt even better when she took all of me in, relaxing her throat enough to give it all to me. I gritted my teeth and tried not to move, but that was a fucking impossibility.

I did it anyway, for her.

"Watching you fuck me with that hot little mouth of yours is going to kill me," I said, smoothing her hair back from her face. "But even knowing that, I don't want you to stop. Go on. Kill me."

Groaning, she sucked harder.

It was official. She was trying to kill me, and she just might succeed.

I moved my hips a little, thrusting into her, and she cupped my balls with her free hand. I knew, right then and there, that I was fucking lost.

And I never wanted to be found again.

Carrie

"Enough," he growled. Catching my hair in his fist, he tugged me to my feet gently. I reluctantly let him, getting one last lick in before I succumbed and stood up. He didn't let go of my hair. My shoulder gave a slight tinge of protest at the movement, but I ignored it. "My turn, Ginger. By the time I'm finished with you, you'll forget how many times I made you come."

"*Yes.*" My stomach tightened in anticipation. "I'm all yours."

His eyes flashed possessively. "Damn right you are."

With a groan, he smashed his mouth down on mine. He backed us toward the bed, his hands cupping my face as he ravished my mouth. I groaned and clung to his forearms, letting him guide me where we needed to go. When the backs of my knees hit the mattress, he followed me. His arms cradled me as he let me fall back on the bed.

Instead of lying on top of me like I'd expected, though, he slid down my body, nipping little patches of skin as he went. My good shoulder. My nipple. My stomach. My hip. And then, oh God...

His mouth closed over me, and his tongue rolled over my clitoris with the perfect amount of pressure. I slung my legs over his shoulders, groaning and gripping the comforter as tight as I could with my right hand. I could feel the tension building up in my belly already. He slid his hands up my body, cupping my breasts, and scraped his thumbs over the hard nipples. When I squirmed and cried out, he did it again. It drove me wilder, each little touch he did, and I knew what I needed. I needed him to claim me.

To make me his.

I tried to lift my hips, straining to get closer to him, but he beat me to it. Without even breaking stride, he cupped my butt with both hands, tipping my hips up. Jackpot, baby. That's what I'd needed—and he'd known it.

His tongue thrashed out again, and I stiffened, so close I could taste it.

"Oh my God," I cried, squeezing my eyes shut. Every nerve in my body tingled, went numb, and then *bam*. I exploded into a million fragments. "Finn," I breathed.

He lowered my hips to the mattress again and slid me fully onto the bed. As he crawled over me again, this time covering my entire length, I let out a happy sigh. For the first time since I'd woken up from my injuries, I felt home. And it felt *amazing*.

"Okay?"

I nodded. "Okay."

He kissed me, and I could taste myself mixed with his own unique flavor on his tongue. His hands roamed everywhere. Touching here. Squeezing there. Instantly, my body came back to life, as if he hadn't just made me have the most explosive orgasm moments before. As if it had been months since I'd had him.

And I needed more.

Slowly, I explored his body. Sliding my hands over all of his black ink, interspersed with a few splashes of color. My name. Our motto. The dates his parents had died. The scars on his upper arm. His wavy light brown hair that begged to be tugged. It was all there to see, and more.

But all I could see, and feel, was this. *Us.*

His fingers dipped between my legs, and I let out a strangled groan. When he thrust a finger inside of me, I screamed, "*Finn!*" I buried my right hand in his hair and yanked hard. "Please. Now."

He moved his fingers inside of me, hitting spots I had forgotten existed, and nibbled on my neck. "Nope. Not yet. You've forgotten one very important thing."

I bit down hard on my lip. "And what would that be?"

"You like to be teased." He scraped his teeth over the swell of my breasts, sliding even lower down my body. "You like when I torture you."

He closed his mouth over my nipple, biting down enough to hurt a little, but not too much. The mixed sensations of pain and pleasure mingling through my veins were addicting. I wanted more. Needed more. "God, yes."

"See?" He smiled and moved lower down my body, nipping skin as he went. When he situated himself between my legs and stared up at me, all possessiveness and desire in his eyes, I sucked in a breath and froze. "And, Ginger, I like making you scream."

He set forth with proving that, because he went down on me again. This time he took his sweet time, moving his tongue with a laziness that drove me insane. By the time he had me perched on the edge again, I was seriously contemplating the best way to murder him for this. But the second I came again, all thoughts of murder were gone.

And I wanted to marry him all over again.

He let me fall back down to the mattress, his muscles bunching with each motion, and he climbed back up my body. When he moved between my legs, I barely had enough energy to blink. But the second he touched his cock to my clitoris, I lost control. Amazingly, I came again, even harder than before.

Tears filled my eyes, because the pleasure was that freaking intense, and I clung to him for dear life. He moved inside of me inch by slow inch, giving me time to adjust if needed. I loved him even more for being concerned for me, for caring, but I needed more. I needed *him*.

Impatiently, I dug my nails into his butt. "God, hurry *up*."

He stiffened and thrust all the way inside me. Once he was completely buried, he froze, his breathing harsh and uneven. His skin was coated with a thin sheen of sweat, and I knew the effort it took to hold himself back was killing him. "Are you okay?"

"Yes." I smacked his arm. "Don't stop. Please, don't stop."

He growled, kissed me, and finally moved with the same passion he always did, while still somehow managing to make sure he didn't jostle my shoulder. Each time he withdrew and came back inside of me, the tension built higher. Stronger. And by the time he stiffened above me, his face lost in the rapturous pleasure of his orgasm, I was there with him again.

With a shuddering sigh, he collapsed on top of me, burying his face in my neck. I hugged him tight, not wanting him to leave me yet, even though I could barely breathe like this. Gently, I trailed my fingers up and down his back. Sometime later, he shuddered and burrowed closer.

"That feels good," he muttered.

"Good. That was my intention."

He snorted. "I'd hope so."

Smiling, I hid my face in his shoulder. "You were right."

"Oh?" He lifted onto his elbows and looked down at me with a furrowed brow. "About what?"

"I totally lost count how many times you made me come."

He kissed the top of my head and grinned cockily. "I know."

"Of course you do." Rolling my eyes, I snuggled in even closer and yawned. "This feels like heaven. I never want to move again."

"Me neither." He hesitated. "But morning will come eventually."

I nodded. "It always does."

"Once you're better, I was thinking we could have your parents watch Susan and take the bike to the beach?" He rose up on his elbows and smoothed my hair back, a tender smile on his face. And his eyes... those eyes shone with so much love for me. "Once you're better, we could maybe even go out in the water for a little bit? It always soothes my mind, so I thought maybe it would be good for you, too."

I leaned up on my elbows, excitement making my heart race. "Oh my God, *yes*."

He smirked. "I think you just said that a few minutes ago."

"Finn." I smacked his arm. "I'm serious."

"I know." He kissed my nose. "We'll go in a few weeks, but not until you're fully healed. But no big waves for you, and you have to promise to listen to me out there. Out there, I am the ruler of the sea. You obey my every command without question. We'll just go out there and get the feel of the waves again."

"I've heard this speech before. I promise that I'll obey your every command in the water." I trailed my hand down his chest. "But out of it..."

He rolled me underneath of him and nipped at my neck. "You still obey me."

"In the bedroom maybe."

"That's all I ask." He kissed me, keeping it light and gentle. I knew he was worried to push me too hard, and it made me feel so cherished and loved. Pulling back, he caressed my cheek with a featherlight touch. His blue eyes shone down on me, and I couldn't help but smile up at him with tears in my eyes. "I love you, Ginger."

"I love you, too," I whispered.

Despite everything we'd seen, everything we'd done, we'd survived. More than that? We'd *lived*. Life would never be easy, and we still had a million obstacles to overcome. There would be a million more, too, I was sure. But love...well...

Love had conquered all.

Epilogue

Carrie

Christmas Eve
One year later

Taking a deep breath, I smoothed my dress, walked through the foyer, and into the living room. The bright tree decorated in colored lights stood in front of the window, and Finn sat on the couch in front of the fireplace with Susan in his lap. Cinnamon potpourri tickled my senses as I came closer.

He read her *The Night Before Christmas*.

She listened intently, her blue eyes locked on the pages and her little hands wrapped around his thumbs. She'd grown so much over the past year—heck, we had, too—and one thing was for certain. She was daddy's girl. Every morning, she woke up calling out for him. And every night, she insisted he be the one to lie her down.

It never failed to make me smile and thank my lucky stars I'd walked out of that party all those years ago and found him. Thank God I'd found him.

"Daddy." She pulled at his thumb. "What's that?"

"A bunny." He kissed her head. "And he's hanging his stocking over the fireplace, just like we do."

I watched them, tears coming to my eyes. Happy tears.

The love they shared was the most pure love I'd ever seen, and I'd never get sick of it. Ever. Finn smiled at me and continued to read the book, doing silly voices as he went along. I grinned, as into the story as Susan was. Maybe even more. I loved it when Finn read out loud.

Especially when he read me one of my romance books.

When he finished the book and closed it, he nuzzled Susan's neck and made snorting noises. She giggled and cried out, "Daddy, no!"

"Stop torturing my baby," I said, walking forward with a big smile on my face.

Finn was doing so much better, and so was I. We'd stopped jumping at loud noises. We confided in each other, making sure we kept each other updated on how we were doing. We were open and honest and happy. *So* happy.

"She likes it," he said in defense, his blue eyes shining. "Right, Susan?"

Susan smiled up at him lovingly.

Sitting beside them, I took a second to appreciate the moment. I'd learned to start doing that, too. "Are you ready for Santa to come?" I asked, laughing when she looked at me with wide eyes. "Or maybe not..."

Finn laughed and hugged her closer. "I don't think she knows who that is yet."

"He'll bring you presents and put them under the tree tonight. When you wake up?" I pointed to the tree with a huge smile. "Everything you could ever want will be there, waiting for you."

She stared at me with wide eyes before turning to Finn. "Daddy too?"

"Of course." When she glanced away, he turned to me. "But what if I already have everything I could ever want right here on this couch with me?"

Susan hopped off his lap and took off, heading for the tree. We'd had to secure it to the wall because she loved to tug on it. My heart stuttered and sped up. "Funny, I have the same issue."

"Hmm..." He leaned in and kissed me, lingering when he pulled away. "Maybe I should put this little princess in bed, and then we could see if we could think of anything else we might like?" Finn asked, his voice low and husky.

I smiled against his lips. "I think I could work with that."

"Good." He stood and stared at Susan, the warm smile on his face going right to my heart. "I'm glad I came home early. It's good to be home."

"We're glad too. We missed you." He'd gone to his coworker's party at a nearby pub. I'd stayed home to watch Susan. And to prepare for the moment that was about to come. "Was there any good food?"

"Yes, so much food it was ridiculous. I brought you home some of those brownies you like. Riley showed up, too, with some Scottish friend of his. I didn't even know he had any Scottish friends."

"Yeah, from college." I smiled. "Wallace, right?"

"Aye," Finn said in a fake Scottish accent. "All the lassies swooned over him."

"I can see why." I trailed my fingers over his chest. "Keep talking in that accent, and I might swoon, too."

"You know what?" He narrowed his eyes on me, dropping the accent. "I don't know whether to be jealous of myself or not."

Laughing, I rolled my eyes. "I vote for *not*."

"We'll see about that." He looked me up and down. "But anyway, half the people were wasted, so I cut out early. I'd rather be here with you guys than watch people drink until they forget their own names. I'm too old for that shit."

I rolled my eyes. "You're not even thirty-three yet. Hardly *that* old."

He bent down, cupped my cheek, and ran his thumb over my lower lip. His tender gaze met mine, and I swear I saw straight to the depths of his very soul. "Thank you."

"For what?" I asked, my breath hitching in my throat.

"For believing in me again."

"Thank you for believing in me, too." I smiled. "I love you."

"I love you, too." He crossed the room, took the red ornament out of Susan's hand, and picked her up. "I'll show you just how much as soon as she's asleep."

"Noooooooooo!" Susan squealed, arching her back. "I'm na tired!"

"Sure you're not, Princess." He kissed her head. "Are her PJs in the crib waiting for us like usual?"

My heart picked up speed, and my legs went weak. He was about to get my early present to him. One I'd only just gotten earlier this morning. "Yep. Mmhmm. It is." I laughed. "I mean *they* are. They're there. Waiting. For you. In the crib."

He eyed me, rocking Susan back and forth in his arms. She smacked his jaw and tried to get down. "O...kay. I'll be right back."

I listened to his footsteps retreat. Once they hit the hallway upstairs, I tiptoed after him. As I crept down the hallway, I heard him talking to Susan about Santa, and presents, and love, and how lucky we all were.

It made me smile, because he was about to feel even luckier.

I know I did.

Through the crack of the door, I watched as he took her Christmas Eve dress off and picked up the pink shirt I'd bought earlier today. The one that told him my news with perfect clarity. He tossed it aside, choosing to put the striped Christmas-themed pants on first.

He was *torturing* me.

After he had the pants in place, he picked up the shirt and pulled it over her head. As he guided her arms through gently, he *tsk*ed and shook his head. "Mommy once told me red and pink don't match. That's why she doesn't own anything pink. Yet look what she got you, also a redhead. A...pink...shirt...that...says..."

When he didn't finish talking, and just stared at Susan, I opened the door the rest of the way. It creaked on the hinges. He didn't turn around.

"'I'm the big sister,'" I supplied. "That's what it says."

"*Carrie.*" He spun on his heel, his eyes soft and tender and excited. "Is it true?"

"It is." I nodded, smiling so big it hurt. "I just took the pregnancy test today. When it came back positive, I rushed out to buy the shirt. I couldn't think of a more perfect time or way to tell you than—"

He strode across the room in three giant steps, swept me up in his arms, and spun me in a huge circle. "Oh my God, Carrie. You're fu—freaking incredible."

I clung to him, squeezing my eyes shut. "Morning sickness!"

"Oops." He stopped spinning me instantly, but didn't set me down. "I love you so much, you know that?"

"I do." I cupped his cheeks. "And I love you, too."

"I know," he said, grinning up at me. "Believe me, I know."

He turned out Susan's light, carried me out the door, and walked right into our bedroom. As soon as he laid me on the bed, he rested his hands on my belly, staring at it in awe. He pushed my shirt up and kissed my stomach. "A baby. Another baby," he whispered. "It's a miracle, Ginger. A fucking miracle. I can't believe how incredible you are. How happy you make me every single day."

I blinked back tears. We'd been trying to get pregnant since I'd lost the other baby. For a while there, I'd thought maybe I couldn't have more children. I'd thought it was something that asshat Kyle had taken from me. Maybe Finn had feared that, too.

But I'd been wrong. We were blessed again.

"You make me happier," I said. "A million times happier."

He shook his head and kissed my stomach again. "Billion."

"Trillion," I whispered, threading my hands into his hair. "Are you happy?"

"So fucking happy." He climbed up my body and lowered his face to mine. "You?"

I grinned. "So much it should hurt."

"You saved me," he said, taking a deep breath. "You saved me so many times."

"You saved me as many times." I tugged on his hair. "We're equal. I'm sure of it."

"Me too." He nipped at my lower lip. "As a matter of fact, I'm positive as a proton about it."

Grinning, I kissed him. "Me too, Finn. Me too."

I smoothed his hair off his face, studying the scars that reminded me of all we'd been through. All we'd survived. All the odds that had been thrown at us and tried to rip us apart, but we hadn't given up. We'd stayed strong and fought for our love. For each other. We'd come out stronger. Better. More in love than ever.

How many people could say the same?

Blurred Lines, an OUT OF LINE book, will be out January 26th, 2015. The book features Riley from the OUT OF LINE series. Enjoy the following sneak peek.

Love, Jen

chapter
one

Riley

I parked my car in the driveway and just sat there, staring up at the house I shared with my fiancée, Sarah. It was dark outside, and somewhere in the distance, a dog barked. It sounded pissed as hell, but that wasn't why I didn't get out of the car. It wasn't why I was sitting here, feeling empty as hell and just as lost.

The truth was, I wasn't going inside because I knew my fiancée wasn't in there alone. I'd seen the car parked down the road, conveniently hidden behind large shrubbery. On any other man, it might have worked. I might not have noticed it when I drove by on my way to my next meeting. But I'd know that fucking car anywhere.

It was Sarah's ex-boss's car.

The same one she'd once dated.

When we'd met, they'd been freshly split up. He'd broken her heart, and she'd sworn him off forever. After that, we'd dated a suitable amount of time. My parents had liked her, and so had I. It had been an arranged marriage of sorts, but in my circles, that wasn't such a strange thing.

Our fathers were political affiliates. We were expected to marry. Once upon a time, I'd hoped to have more. I'd hoped to have the kind of love that consumed your soul.

I hadn't found it.

So, I'd asked her to marry me. She'd said yes. I'd thought she loved me. I'd been fairly certain I would grow to love her. But if she really loved me...

Why the hell was her ex-boyfriend's car outside my house?

Slowly, I opened my car door and made my way up the driveway. My heart thudded in my ears, and I knew what I'd find when I opened that door. There was no doubt my fiancée was naked and doing the nasty with another man.

And yet, I went inside anyway.

The door creaked when it opened, and I froze, half expecting to hear frantic shouting and retreating footsteps. Nothing moved. I crept inside the rest of the way, leaving the front door open. As I walked, I found a man's sweater on the floor. I stepped on it. Another step and I scored a pair of men's pants and a skirt.

There was no doubt anymore, if there ever had been, that my fiancée was cheating on me. I didn't need to go any farther. I had confirmation. But still...

I kept going.

For some reason, I needed to see it with my own eyes to believe it. I'd truly thought Sarah was an honest woman. One who wouldn't sleep with someone behind my back. I'd thought she would be a good partner for life. A trustworthy one.

I reached the couch. The couch I'd picked out.

Sarah was kneeling between her ex's feet. She was naked, and so was her ex. The man's bare ass was on *my* fucking couch. I didn't know what upset me more: that, or the fact that she was giving the dude a BJ.

She never did that with me. Said it was undignified.

So was fucking a dude on my couch.

And, yes, I knew that the fact that those two things bothered me just as much as the actual betrayal did was fucked up. But I hadn't loved her. I'd wanted to...

But I didn't really know what real love felt like.

Fisting my hands, I cleared my throat. "I'm home early."

Sarah shrieked and flew to her feet, grabbing the throw blanket off the arm of my couch and covering her body with it. Which was absurd, really. We'd both seen her naked before, *obviously*. The man also stood, grabbing a pillow and covering his half-hard dick with it.

"You can keep that now," I said drily, not taking my eyes off Sarah. She was pale and shaking. I forced myself to remain calm. To act as if this hadn't completely taken me off guard, even if it hadn't broken me like it should have. "So, I take it the engagement is off, then?"

"Riley, I'm so sorry." Tears streamed down her cheeks. "I didn't want you to see this…"

"Obviously," I said. "Cheaters rarely do."

She shook her head, her blonde hair flying everywhere. "No. I'm not a cheater. I just—"

"Seriously?" I threw my arms out. "If this isn't cheating, what the hell do you call it?"

Her cheeks flushed. "I love him, Riley. Actually, *really* love him."

I froze then, the unforgettable knowledge that she'd felt the same way about me that I felt about her—and I hadn't even known it. I'd naïvely thought she actually loved me, instead of just, well, accepting me as a suitable partner. How had I missed that?

"I thought you loved me," I said softly, scratching my head. "I didn't know…"

"I do." She came up to me, resting her hand on my heart. The same hand that had been cupping another man's balls moments before. That skeeved me out. "I love you, Riley."

"But you're not in love with me," I said, swallowing hard.

I might not love her till my dying breath, but the reality of what was happening had hit me pretty hard. We'd been together for three fucking years, and it was over now. We'd just mailed the wedding invitations out last week.

And she'd been fucking him.

"I'm sorry," she whispered, tears falling down her cheeks.

I had no doubt she was. She'd always been a nice person, which was why this came as such a shock. I'd never suspected this of her. Hell, we'd made love last night, and she'd spent half an hour talking about wedding dresses and centerpieces.

I locked eyes with her bright green ones. "When did this start?"

"Riley…"

"*When?*"

She crumbled. "A week ago."

The dude finally spoke up. He took a step forward. "Look, man, I'm sorry, but—"

Without thinking, I cocked my fist back and punched him right in the fucking face. He'd broken her heart, and now he was going to do it again. She might think he'd changed, but any man who would fuck another man's fiancée on his own couch was not a changed man. He was scum, pure and simple.

And she'd fallen for him again.

"Don't speak to me," I snarled. I went after him, even though he stumbled backward and tripped over a fallen pillow. "Don't you ever fucking—"

"Riley, don't!" Sarah called out, sobbing. "Please. Don't hurt him."

I fisted my hands, my breathing coming out harsh. She'd cheated on me with this lowlife, and she was worried I'd hurt him? I whirled on her. "If you loved me, even if you weren't in love with me, you wouldn't have done this, Sarah. Not to me."

She covered her face and cried. "I'm sorry."

"Yeah." I shook my head. "You made a big mistake, Sarah. I would have treated you right. I never would have...never...I wouldn't have done this."

"But you don't love me," she whispered. "You never have."

"I care about you. I respect you." I looked at her again. "I would have treated you right."

"I know," she said, shrugging hopelessly. "I wanted more, though."

And she thought she'd find it with this guy? I looked at him again. He sat on the floor, butt-assed naked and shaking. Pathetic. Turning my attention back to her, I forced a calm smile. My lawyer smile, as I liked to call it.

The one that said: *I have no problem with taking your ass to court and whooping it publicly, so you better enter a plea bargain.* I'd never given it to her before.

"Well, then, I wish you the best of luck. Goodbye."

Sarah stumbled after me, grabbing my arm. "Wait. What will we tell everyone?"

"Tell them whatever you want." I shook off her hold. "I don't care."

She grabbed for me again, but I pulled back. "But—"

"I said I don't fucking care, okay?" I held my hands up. "You were right about one thing—I never loved you. So, I don't give a damn what you say to them."

She covered her mouth and cried. I felt nothing. Not really.

But I didn't want her touching me. Not anymore. This was the second time I'd found my significant other in bed with another man. The first time had been in college, and it had hurt like hell. I'd actually loved her...or I'd thought I had, anyway.

Now I was starting to think I was incapable of love.

I'd loved a girl once, but she hadn't loved me. She'd been in love with her now-husband, and they were the only couple I knew that was actually in love. Like, the kind you see in movies. Finn and Carrie had it, but I never would. Not in this lifetime.

I stumbled out the door, tugging on my tie as I went. It felt tight. As if it had come to life and decided to choke what little life I had left out of me. I was tempted to let it.

I was stuck in a job I hated, in a firm my father owned, and now I was single, too. And for the second time in my life, I'd been duplicitously cheated on.

Was it something I'd done? Something that was missing in me that made my women look elsewhere for something? Maybe I was broken. Maybe I should stop trying to find a partner and just accept the fact that I was better off alone.

Maybe I should just stop trying.

But first? I'd call off my meeting that I was already late to…and I'd get drunk as hell as quickly as possible. I'd get so drunk that I'd forget all about Sarah and the naked man on my couch. So drunk that I'd forget all about how broken I was…

And how I should really be more upset about this whole fucking mess.

Watch for Blurred Lines, out January 26th, 2015.

about the author

Jen McLaughlin is the New Times and USA Today bestselling author of sexy New Adult books. Under her pen name Diane Alberts, she is a multi-published, bestselling author of Contemporary Romance with Entangled Publishing. Her first release as Jen McLaughlin, Out of Line, released September 6, 2013, hit the New York Times, USA Today and Wall Street Journal list. She was mentioned in Forbes alongside E. L. James as one of the breakout independent authors to dominate the bestselling lists. She is represented by Louise Fury at The Bent Agency.

Though she lives in the mountains, she really wishes she was surrounded by a hot, sunny beach with crystal-clear water. She lives in Northeast Pennsylvania with her four kids, a husband, a schnauzer mutt, and a cat. Her goal is to write so many well-crafted romance books that even a non-romance reader will know her name.

This paperback interior was designed and formatted by

E.M. TIPPETTS
BOOK DESIGNS

www.emtippettsbookdesigns.com

Artisan interiors for discerning authors and publishers.

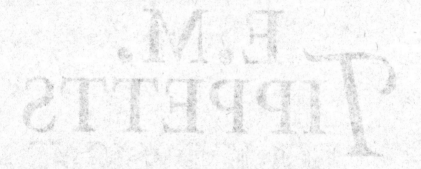